# The Unsigned Valentine

# By Johanna Hurwitz

The Adventures of Ali Baba Bernstein
Aldo Applesauce
Aldo Ice Cream
Aldo Peanut Butter
Ali Baba Bernstein, Lost and Found
Baseball Fever
Birthday Surprises: Ten Great Stories to Unwrap
Busybody Nora
Class Clown
Class President
The Cold & Hot Winter
Dear Emma
DeDe Takes Charge!
The Down & Up Fall
"E" Is for Elisa
Elisa in the Middle
Elisa Michaels, Bigger & Better
Even Stephen
Ever-Clever Elisa
Faraway Summer
Fourth-Grade Fuss
The Hot & Cold Summer
Hurray for Ali Baba Bernstein
Hurricane Elaine
The Just Desserts Club
The Law of Gravity
A Llama in the Family

Llama in the Library
Make Room for Elisa
Much Ado About Aldo
New Neighbors for Nora
New Shoes for Silvia
Nora and Mrs. Mind-Your-Own-Business
Once I Was a Plum Tree
One Small Dog
Ozzie on His Own
The Rabbi's Girls
Rip-Roaring Russell
Roz and Ozzie
Russell and Elisa
Russell Rides Again
Russell Sprouts
Russell's Secret
School's Out
School Spirit
Spring Break
Starting School
Summer with Elisa
Superduper Teddy
Teacher's Pet
Tough-Luck Karen
The Up & Down Spring
A Word to the Wise: And Other Proverbs
Yellow Blue Jay

# The Unsigned Valentine

## And Other Events in the Life of Emma Meade

JOHANNA HURWITZ

*Illustrated by Mary Azarian*

HARPERCOLLINS*PUBLISHERS*

Library of Congress Cataloging-in-Publication Data
Hurwitz, Johanna.
    The unsigned valentine : and other events in the life of Emma Meade /
Johanna Hurwitz ; illustrated by Mary Azarian.— 1st ed.
        p.   cm.
    Summary: In early twentieth-century Vermont, sixteen-year-old Emma confides
in her diary both her hopes of becoming a farmer's wife one day and her frustrations
with her parents' belief that she is too young to be courted by the handsome Cole
Berry.
    ISBN-10: 0-06-056053-3 — ISBN-10: 0-06-056054-1 (lib. bdg.)
    ISBN-13: 978-0-06-056053-9 — ISBN-13: 978-0-06-056054-6 (lib. bdg.)
    [1. Farm life—Vermont—Fiction.  2. Family life—Vermont—Fiction.
3. Courtship—Fiction.  4. Diaries—Fiction.  5. Vermont—History—20th
century—Fiction.]  I. Azarian, Mary, ill.  II. Title.
PZ7.H9574Uns 2006                                              2005006856
[Fic]—dc22                                                          CIP
                                                                    AC

Typography by Larissa Lawrynenko
1  2  3  4  5  6  7  8  9  10
❖
First Edition

Fiona, I love you,
I'll say it again.
Fiona, I love you,
And here's my name—

❧ Nana Johanna

How is it that the individual hours move so slowly and yet the days fly away? All spring our family looked forward to the Sunday in May when Elizabeth Greene, who calls herself "Libby," would change her last name when she married my older brother Edward. Mama and I were very busy as we sewed new shirts for Eddie and for Papa and my brother Tim, too. We also made new dresses for all the women in our family: Mama; my little sister, Nell, who is nine; and, of course, one for me, too. I'm Emma, and I'll be sixteen on my next birthday. When all the sewing was completed, it was time to begin baking. We made many cakes and pies and cookies for

1

the guests to eat at the wedding party.

We talked and prepared for the wedding for such a long time, and yet that celebration on a Sunday in 1911 was over in the blink of an eye. Then we began to plan for a return visit from Hadassah Rabinowitz, the Fresh Air girl who lives in New York City and visited with us last summer. Dossi had never seen a farm before and all that goes with it: cows; chickens; our pig; Dandy, our horse; and everything else. Her amazement at everything during her first visit made me begin to look at my life with a new appreciation.

Dossi returned here on the first of August. We did all the things we did last year: picnics down by the pond and swimming on hot days. There was not one drop of rain during the two weeks that Dossi was staying here, and there had been no rain for weeks before, either. So each day the pond grew smaller and smaller. Finally we were just wetting our toes and coming out with them covered in mud.

"When my feet are cool, the rest of my body hardly feels the heat at all," Dossi said. She was very happy being with us, and nothing seemed to disappoint or discourage her. Still, Dossi spoke a lot about the coming school year. She is about to begin high school, and she's excited about her new studies. She secretly hopes to go on to college and to become a doctor.

"Don't you want to do something special with your life?" she asked me more than once.

Even though we've become great friends, confiding in each other, I think Dossi finds my satisfaction with everyday life hard to understand. I will be very content to marry and have children, to run a farm and do all the things my mother has done before me. "It's hard to explain the pleasure I feel when I look at the shelves of canned food at the end of the summer," I told her. "I know that we grew the vegetables and fruits, that we picked and prepared them ourselves. And the rows of jars mean that once again we have met the challenge of staving off hunger for another year."

"But don't you want anything *more*?" Dossi asked.

"There is one thing," I said slowly.

"Yes?" she asked, encouraging me to tell her what it was.

"I could run a farm, raise a family, and still do one other thing," I told her.

"And what is it?"

"I would like to help develop our town library. Now it's just a spare room in Miss Peabody's home and open only two days a week. If I helped her, it could be open other days. And more important, maybe I could figure out a way to get extra books. Most of the books now are gifts from the townspeople. It's very exciting when the library gets a single new book. I want to make the town council set up a fund so new books can be bought regularly."

"Good for you," said Dossi, squeezing my arm. "You can do it."

"Well, not yet," I said, blushing at her enthusiasm. "The council won't pay attention to me now. They'd say I had nothing better to do with my time than sit around and read. But reading is important."

"Of course it is," Dossi agreed. "I love to read."

"I want to encourage everyone in town to feel the way we do. There could be a book club to discuss books. Everyone would be welcome. Women could bring their needlework to keep

4

their fingers busy while we talk. And if we served some tea and cake, it would encourage many nonreaders to come and listen. People will sit through all sorts of things for a slice of cake that someone else baked."

"Especially if it's a cake that you or your mother made," said Dossi. "You are a wonderful cook."

And so with household chores, walks, and berry picking, Dossi's visit passed quickly. One day stands out in my memory. It was too hot for walking or berry picking. We didn't know what to do. Mama had just baked some loaves of bread, and she suggested that we go and visit Libby. "This raisin bread is Eddie's favorite," she reminded me. "I'm sure he'll be pleased to have it, and Libby will be delighted to have some company."

Nell had already planned to play with the Thomas sisters, who live nearby, and so Dossi and I went off on our own. As Mama had thought, Libby was happy to see us. She showed off her wedding china and her new linens. We admired the chest and the table and chairs that she and Eddie had bought. Their bed is covered with the rose wreath quilt that Mama and I pieced together for the wedding couple during the winter.

Libby served us iced tea and sliced some of the raisin loaf to serve with it. We talked together until suddenly Libby let out a shout. "I know what I must do," she said. Dossi and I looked at her. We had no idea what she was talking about.

"Dossi, you have the most beautiful hair I've ever seen," said Libby, stroking my friend's red-dish blond hair. "But the style you have is much too severe. You have such a high forehead. You would look much better if you let me cut a fringe."

I turned to see if Dossi was offended by my sister-in-law's words. After all, one doesn't expect to walk into someone's home and be told one needs to cut one's hair to improve one's appearance.

"Why not?" asked Dossi, laughing. "Go ahead," she told Libby.

"Dossi. You don't have to let her do it," I said nervously. I like my new sister-in-law, but I had already learned that Libby has a very heavy hand when it comes to pastry. I didn't trust her with my friend's hair.

"It's only hair. If I don't like it, I can let it

grow back. But it will be fun to go home and to start my new school with a new look. Yes, go ahead. Do it right now," she instructed Libby.

And so Libby cleared the dishes from the table and put a towel around Dossi's neck. Then she took her scissors from her workbasket and her comb from the top of the chest of drawers.

I held my breath as Libby began snipping away. There was no more talking. We were all quiet during this operation. Suddenly Dossi let out a loud sneeze. "The hair is tickling my nose," she said, giggling. Libby and I laughed too.

Believe me, no one was more amazed than I at how beautiful Dossi was when Libby finished her job. The fringe somehow managed to emphasize the blue of her eyes. Her nose looked smaller too, as if Libby had cut off a piece of that as well. Libby ran and got her hand mirror for Dossi to see the result. "Is that really me?" she asked. We assured her it was.

"Now you must transform me as well," I insisted to Libby.

"I would love to cut your hair," she said. "But I don't dare touch it without your mother's consent. She won't scold me for cutting Dossi's hair, but I don't know how she'd feel if you returned home with a new look too." I knew Libby was right, and so I didn't protest. After all, I would have many other opportunities to let her cut my hair now that I knew about this skill of hers.

There was a little breeze as we walked back to our farmhouse later that afternoon. We hoped the heat wave was breaking up and maybe there would even be some much-needed rain. When we reached home, we didn't say a word but waited to see the reaction from my family. I was surprised that Mama said nothing. I didn't expect Papa to comment on Dossi's new hairstyle. But when we sat down to supper, Tim asked at once, "Is this the same young lady who had breakfast here this morning?"

Poor Dossi turned as red as a beet. And Nell, who for once had held her tongue, began to beg Mama to let Libby cut her hair too. "Dossi is a young woman and you are still a little girl," Mama told Nell. I didn't say anything about my hair, but I'll get Mama to consent yet.

Now Dossi has gone back to New York City, and September is almost here.

🌿 Friday, September 1, 1911

*H*ot, sunny day. Feather clouds above.

It wasn't even my birthday when Mama gave me this blank book to use as a journal. I think she must have bought it when she went shopping in Burlington with Papa last week. She said she saw me writing so much that she guessed it would be a good gift. Perhaps she's right. I seem to find it much easier to record my thoughts than to say them aloud. Last winter when the Vermont senate rejected full voting rights for women, I heard many people voice their opinions. At a church social shortly after the vote was written up in the newspaper, almost all the women had something to say about the situation. I was shocked how many said it was right for only men to vote in state and national elections. They said women have enough to do with all their housework and gardening chores. Why should they fill up their heads with political problems as well? I didn't comment at all. But I sat down and wrote an angry letter of protest to the editor of Papa's newspaper. I watched the paper for a couple of weeks and was disappointed that my letter wasn't printed. But at least I'm sure that the editor read it. And I felt better for having expressed myself.

Nell is just the opposite of me. She thinks out loud and is never silent. She could talk the tin ear off an iron dog. Mama constantly tells her, "Speak less, say more." But Nell, like so many other people, usually speaks more and says less. She is worse than the endless droning of bees in the summer.

But I keep silent and sometimes write my words on paper. Until now, the writing I've done is school assignments and letters to Dossi.

When a letter arrives here from Dossi, it's always exciting. If I've come home from a day at school or from hours of helping Papa and Tim with the chores, the sight of a new envelope from Dossi lifts my spirits and gives me so much to chew over in my mind. It's better than a new book borrowed from the library! Life in New York City is so different and interesting. Life here in Jericho is exactly the same, day after day. I'm not complaining, but now that I spend so much time helping with farm work, it's harder than ever to find things to write about to Dossi. I wondered aloud to my mother, as I wrote *EMMA MEADE* on the cover, what in the world I'll find to fill up the pages.

"Emma Meade," Mama scolded. "Who knows what will happen next? No matter how tough the roast beef, you can always cut the gravy with your knife," she told me. Now what is that supposed to mean?

I find writing easier than speaking aloud. No one can laugh at me. I'm happier observing life around me than discussing it with another person. And for some reason, in my letters to Dossi, I notice that I can share my ideas more easily than I can when we sit face-to-face.

At the moment all anyone around here is talking about is rain. We had hardly enough to drown a flea this summer. So it's incredible that we grew any crops at all. We were constantly taking pails of water out to the vegetable garden. And Mama saved the dishwater and the dirty bathwater to pour on the plants, too. Now Papa has been worrying about the water in the well. Several neighbors have complained that their wells are running dry, and we may be the next to have this problem.

"Don't worry. I'll drink milk instead of water," said Nell. "Or I can drink the fresh cider we are making," she said, referring to the barrels of juice we've just begun squeezing out of our apple crop.

"I suppose you'll wash your face and hands in milk or cider too?" I asked her.

Nell laughed at that. She thought it was funny. But I know that when a well goes dry, it's not funny at all. Perhaps we'll have to dig again and hope to find more water.

## Sunday, September 10, 1911

Another hot, dry day, feather clouds, six weeks since our last rain.

At noon Eddie and Libby came back to the house with us to have dinner, after church. At Mama's instruction, I had laid the table using our best cloth with the embroidered flowers on it. It's funny to think we have to impress Libby now that she is Libby Meade, and part of our family. And it's strange to treat Eddie like he is special company and not my older brother who had lived with us all his life until his wedding. When he was courting Libby, Mama used to look at Eddie and tease, "Love and a cough cannot be hidden."

Today Mama had prepared all of Eddie's favorite dishes, as if it was his birthday. He came dressed in his dark wedding suit and looked very formal, but the day was so hot that he quickly removed his jacket and rolled up his shirtsleeves. Then, as he sat at our table eating Mama's chicken fricassee and drinking buttermilk with his apple pie, he looked more like the brother I always knew.

Libby wore her blue calico print dress. Usually it makes the blue of her eyes stand out, but today she looked peaked and worn. It seemed to me that this was not the way an eighteen-year-old bride of four months should look. She poked at her food and hardly ate more than a few mouthfuls. I looked at my mother and wondered if she felt hurt after all her work to make this meal so perfect. Personally I've tasted some of Libby's mother's food at church socials, and I don't think she's nearly as good a cook as my mother.

At first there wasn't much talking at the table. Then Nell, who can never keep quiet for long, looked across at Eddie and said, "I have a new riddle for you. How many feet have forty sheep, a shepherd, and a dog?"

Mama, Papa, Tim, and I had all been tricked by this riddle when Nell first asked it earlier in the week. So we kept silent while Eddie did the arithmetic in his head.

He swallowed his mouthful of food and answered, "A hundred sixty-six," just as each of us had responded.

"Wrong, wrong!" shouted Nell with glee.

"There's just two because only a shepherd has feet. The sheep have hooves, and the dog has paws."

Eddie laughed good-naturedly. He'd already been tricked by Nell a hundred times in the past.

Suddenly Libby jumped up from the table and rushed to the privy. Eddie's face turned red at his wife's departure.

"Is everything all right?" Mama asked him. "Is she ill?"

Eddie turned redder still. But when Libby returned, he looked at her and she nodded. Then he cleared his throat and made an announcement.

"Libby and I want to tell you that it seems she is going to become a mother," he said.

Nell let out a shriek before the news had quite sunk in for the rest of us. "I'm going to be an aunt!" she crowed. She jumped up from the table and pranced about the room. "Aunt Nell," she said. "Or maybe I should be called by my real name: Aunt Eleanor." Once again Nell's nine-year-old childishness served a purpose. We all laughed at her, and it gave poor Libby a chance to compose herself.

By the end of the meal, the new parents and grandparents-to-be, future aunts, and Uncle Tim were all talking busily about the things one usually discusses on a farm: the weather, with its lack of rain; the crops; the livestock; and plans for next year. Eddie works a piece of land adjacent to that owned by Libby's father. Mr. Greene bought the land a few years back but had never gotten around to cultivating it. Libby's father built a small house in one corner of the property for his daughter and her husband. As Libby is an only child, someday both farms will belong to her and Eddie. The neighbors say he married well because of the land. I say he married well because he loves Libby.

"If only it would snow," said Tim. "Then all our water problems would be over."

"Snow?" I gasped. "I've never heard anyone wish for snow. It always comes too soon," I said, thinking of all the October snows I've lived through.

"And it stays much longer than we want," added Libby. She was thinking of the April storms we often have.

"I love snow!" exclaimed Nell. "It's so much

fun to play in it and to go sledding."

But to the men sitting around our table, there was no thought of playing. Snow is another form of water, and that's what all the farms need now.

Tim told how he'd attempted to go fishing earlier in the week. "It was so dry that the fish kicked up an awful dust getting upstream," he quoted. That's a saying we've all heard before. This time, however, I believe it's not a joke, but almost the truth! And of course, with little water in the lake, there were no fish, either.

When the meal ended, Papa and my brothers went out to check the well. Mama took Libby off to show her some fabric scraps that she has. Libby wants to piece a quilt for the baby. As for Nell and me, we were left to finish clearing the table and wash the dishes. Although I'm not afraid of work, dish washing is one job I truly dislike. After working hard to prepare a meal, I like to sit still for a while after eating. I wish there were a magical way that the dishes could wash themselves. When I told that to Mama once, she said, "I thought Nell was my fanciful daughter, not you. You're supposed to be the sensible one, with your feet planted firmly on the ground. Stop

17

building castles in the air and wishing for the impossible. It's a waste of energy. Wishes won't wash dishes."

It was Tim who said to me, "Cheer up. Someday you'll have a daughter who you can tell to wash the dishes."

Mama laughed at that.

I occupied my mind during the drudgery of washing pots and dishes by trying to imagine what it would feel like to have a baby growing inside of me. But it was impossible for me to conceive such a sensation.

# BURLINGTON FREE PRESS

## *SEPTEMBER 18, 1911*

Records show that the entire Northeast has received less than the normal average rainfall. Northern Vermont received only .2 of an inch of rain during August. July brought only .25 inches of rain. The average rainfall during these months is usually 3 inches. Although everyone enjoyed the cloudless, dry summer days, we are now beginning to suffer from the effects of the drought. Farmers all over New England are complaining that their fields are parched. Wells are drying up. Brooks and streams are now merely mud puddles.

It is hoped that heavy snows will help saturate the earth in the months ahead.

Hot, dry. Not a single cloud in the sky.

Life on a farm is hard. In the summer we worried that it would rain before we brought in the hay. We were lucky. Tim and Papa managed to bale 215 loads of hay without a drop of rain to harm it. Then when the haying was done, we wanted that water. But now it's been two months, and all we had was about seven drops of rain a few days ago. And worst of all, the well is running dry. The water is muddy, and we need to let it set after it's pumped up so that the dirt will fall to the bottom. Mama says not to drink it until it's been boiled, but we still use it for washing. Even muddy water is better than none, she reminds us.

Today a dowser named Earl Peck, who lives south of here in East Charlotte, came to see if he could locate another source of water on our property. Papa had been trying to get him to come for several weeks, but we're not the only ones having water problems, so we had to wait our turn. I guess being a dowser is like being a farmer; you depend a lot on weather. But no rain is good for *his* business, even though it's bad for ours.

Farmers work hard—digging, lifting, milking, plowing. It takes a lot of physical strength. Mr. Peck only has to walk about holding a witch-hazel branch shaped like a Y. He held one short end of the branch in his right hand and the other in his left.

"See, I grasp it firmly," he told us. (We were standing by and watching him. Even Mama, who complained she was as busy as a one-eyed cat watching two rat holes, left the kitchen to see what was going to happen.) The crotch of the branch stood vertically up in the air.

Mr. Peck walked about, up and down the yard, past the vegetable patch, toward the barn and the fields, and around again.

"It's like magic," Nell whispered to me as we followed him.

"He hasn't found anything yet," I replied. I worried. Suppose there was no other under-ground spring to supply water on our property? Mr. Peck walked slowly and thoughtfully. Still nothing happened. Then suddenly, about a hundred yards off on the far side of our house, the branch moved in Mr. Peck's hands and the Y of the branch tipped downward.

I hadn't realized I'd been holding my breath. But at that moment, I let it out with a loud sigh of relief.

"The harder the crotch tips downward, the more water there is. And this is a lulu!" Mr. Peck exclaimed.

"Can I try it?" Nell begged.

"Why sure, little lady," Mr. Peck replied. He handed his divining rod to her.

Nell stood just at the spot where Mr. Peck had been. She put a hand around each end and waited for the crotch to point downward. Nothing happened. "It doesn't want to go down again," she complained.

"Not everyone can find water like I can. I have some sort of electricity in my body that does it. I've had it since I was a lad," he explained. "I was just born with it."

"Like singing," Mama said. "Some can carry a tune and some can't."

"Well, I can sing, even if I can't find water," said Nell, returning the branch to Mr. Peck.

"If we dig a well here and find good, sweet

water, we'll all have something to sing about,"
Papa said with a big grin on his face. I know he
was very relieved by even the thought of more
water on our property.

"Anyone else want to try?" Mr. Peck asked.
He held out his branch. "It helps if you concen-
trate on water. Don't think about fixing lunch,"
he said to Mama, "or the price you'll get for your
milk." This was meant for Papa. I was tempted,
but I didn't want to be shown up as incompetent
like Nell had been.

"You've got a good reputation for finding
water," Papa said. "If you say this is the spot, I
want to start work on it as soon as I can. I'll pay
your fee, and I'll play with your branch another
day."

"You'll find it," Mr. Peck assured Papa. "Else
I'll give you your money back. I've only failed
once in all the years I've been searching for
water, and that was because the man didn't dig
exactly where I'd told him to."

Within the hour Tim and Papa had the pick
and shovel out and were working away. Vermont
soil grows more rocks than crops, so digging is
very slow and hard labor. Even though I've been

doing more and more chores around the farm since Eddie got married, this was one job that I was glad not to have to do. I got some water that had been boiled earlier in the day. I put some chips of ice in it and gave it to them to drink. Both Tim and Papa were already drenched in sweat.

"I don't know if I should pour this over my head or have a drink," Tim said when I gave him a cup. His face was flushed and streaked with dirt.

"If you drink it, it will just come out of your body in a few minutes," I told him. "I'll milk all the cows tonight," I offered. It was the least I could do.

*S*lightly cooler but still no rain.

There was a pie social at church Saturday evening. All the women brought pies and all the men (and the women and children, too) ate them. There was the usual variety of fillings: rhubarb, strawberry, cherry, custard, mince, apple, apple crumb, peach, peach crumb, lemon, blueberry, and blackberry. Some of the pies were mixed, like strawberry rhubarb, or apple blackberry. In the end, however, a good pie depends not on its filling but on its crust. Mama has taught me how to make a flaky crust that doesn't get soggy from the fruit, and browns to a pleasing shade without burning.

Eddie and Libby were there. Libby still looks peaked to me, but now that I know the reason, I don't worry about it. It occurred to me that Libby isn't so very much older than me. I wonder if two years from now I'll be a married woman too? Almost at the very moment that thought passed through my head, someone bumped into me. Luckily I'd already placed the apple pie that

I'd been holding onto the large rectory table. Otherwise I'm sure I would have dropped it.

I turned to see who it was and there was Cole Berry. He's a friend of Eddie's and works at odd jobs around town. He's very tall and handsome. I first met him last spring when Libby and Eddie got married. Because he'd worked for Libby's father for a time, he was one of the guests at the wedding party. Cole's got the bluest eyes I've ever seen. My heart beats rapidly whenever I see him, and I have to remind myself that Handsome apples are sometimes sour.

"Cole. You just missed having apple pie on your pants and shoes," I told him. "One second earlier and you'd have had to eat your dessert straight off your clothing."

"If you'd baked it, I'd eat it off the ground," said Cole.

Now that's a funny compliment, if you ask me. It almost sounded as if he was sweet on me, but I suppose he's just fond of pies.

"I'm pleased to know which of those pies you brought tonight," he added. "I'm sure if you baked it, it's sweet and good."

"Even if I brought a vinegar pie?" I asked.

Vinegar pie is imitation lemon, which one can make when the general store doesn't have any lemons in stock.

"Vinegar pie is my very favorite. I'd eat it with relish," Cole asserted.

"Pickle relish with vinegar. Oooh. That would be too sour for my taste," I told him.

"You implied that you'd brought apple pie," said Cole. "So I don't have to prove my words this evening."

I didn't know how to respond. I felt my face getting hotter, and I looked down at the table covered with pies. I felt as awkward as a cow with a wooden leg. I pretended to be studying them all as if one could learn something from looking at a piece of pastry. Well, I guess in a way you could. Some were burnt along the edges but not mine. I'd made a lattice crust on top, and it had come out perfectly.

"Well, see you around," said Cole. He winked at me and walked away.

I stood for a moment, annoyed at myself. I wished I could have said something witty and clever that would have held Cole's attention and kept him talking with me a bit longer. But then I realized that I'd just exchanged more words with Cole than the sum total of all I'd said to him during the four hours of the wedding party. Come to think of it, he'd said more to me, too, so that cheered me up a little.

I went over to sit with Libby. Nell came and joined us. She was disappointed that her friends Alyssa and Jenna hadn't come to church this evening. I was disappointed too, because it meant that Libby and I had to listen to Nell try her latest tongue twisters on us instead of her friends.

"The cat ran over the roof of the house with a lump of raw liver in her mouth." And "Six slick, slim saplings."

Cole walked over, and for a few minutes he succeeded in repeating Nell's tongue twisters. I think it was sweet of him to humor my little sister. Then Josephine Wheeler, whose father owns the mill, came and pulled Cole away. "I want to show you something," she said to him. So off he went.

I noticed that there was a very lively and attractive woman sitting nearby among a group of congregation members. She stood out like a blackberry in a pan of milk. I didn't recognize her, and I asked Libby if she knew who she was.

"That's Mrs. Grace Coolidge. I heard she's originally from the Burlington area, but now she lives in Massachusetts. She's here visiting for a few days with Mrs. Goodhue, who's her cousin," Libby told me. She pointed out the woman's two young sons, who were eyeing the pies impatiently. "Someone said her husband's a Vermonter. But now he's a big lawyer in Springfield, Massachusetts, and he's running for state senator there."

Eddie came over to speak with Libby, and I excused myself. I was curious about Mrs. Coolidge. She was holding everyone's attention by moving her hands in a strange way and speaking at the same time. I moved toward my mother, who was among the onlookers. "Mrs. Coolidge worked in a school for the deaf before she was married," Mama explained to me. "She's showing how deaf people can communicate without sound. It's called sign language."

It was fascinating to watch Mrs. Coolidge's hand signals.

"This means *I'm happy to be here*," Mrs. Coolidge said, moving her fingers.

"How would you say *I love you?*" someone asked her.

That started a whole list of requests. But though she could converse with her hands, our guest was just as busy talking with her mouth. She told about the students and how happy they were to speak with one another. "You should see some of them in church," she said. "They gossip and chatter just like naughty children," she reported. "Only of course they don't disturb others because it is all silent."

Many in Mrs. Coolidge's audience moved their fingers in imitation of her. "It's important to remember," our visitor said, "that just because a person has been inflicted with deafness does not mean that they are not intelligent. My students at Clarke were bright and eager to learn. And not just the sign language; they wanted to know all school subjects. Some even went on to college."

"How do you say *I'm getting mighty hungry?*" called out old Mrs. Caldwell. Everyone laughed at that.

Just then Mrs. Bentley rang the bell that summoned us to the tables. We bowed our heads, right where we stood, as the minister recited a brief prayer of thanksgiving. Then everyone rushed toward the food. I smiled at Mrs. Coolidge, who suddenly stood alone without her audience.

"One can't compete with a good pie," I said to her by way of apology.

"I wouldn't even try," she said, holding out her hand in greeting. "What is your name, my dear?" she asked.

I told her. And then I said shyly, "I admire your social skills. If I was in a room with so many people I had never seen before, I would not be able to say a word. Why, I know everyone here and I can hardly talk."

"Well, it seems to me you're doing a fine job of it," said Mrs. Coolidge, putting her arm through mine as we moved toward the food. "But I'll tell you something, my dear. My husband is a quiet man who doesn't speak much either. We make a fine team together. Speakers always need listeners. Even my deaf students need someone to see their words. I bet you are a fine listener. So don't belittle yourself."

I blushed at her compliment and didn't know how to respond. Then she added, "Besides, if you don't spend all your time gabbing away, then when you do have something to say, people will really pay attention to you. And that's good."

I couldn't imagine ever having anything really important to say to anyone and was just about to tell her that when her cousin grabbed her arm. "Grace," she said, "I've saved a seat for you. Come with me."

Mrs. Coolidge turned and smiled at me. "Don't forget what I said," she told me.

I moved toward a table where my parents were sitting with Eddie and Libby. Everyone was busy eating as if this was the first time they had tasted anything sweet in weeks. I looked for Cole Berry. He was sitting with several young men and women. I noticed that he ate not one, but two slices of my apple pie.

I felt very proud until I saw him later talking and laughing with Josie Wheeler as he ate a piece of her blueberry pie. I wonder if I missed him eating any other pies. He sure has a big appetite for such a lean fellow.

A bit later I saw Cole, his lips still stained with blueberries, talking with Tim and Papa. He caught my eye and winked at me. I looked for

Mrs. Coolidge to bid her good-bye, but I didn't see her. She must have departed early because of her two young sons. It occurred to me that since she lives in Springfield, she might know Mama's sister who lives there. But maybe not. Springfield is a large city, not a small town like Jericho.

On the way home, Papa said that Eddie and Cole were going to come by on Wednesday to help with the well digging. I'm glad. He and Tim have been working much too hard and need all the help they can get to reach water. Papa had the three dollars to pay Mr. Peck for his dowsing work, but he doesn't have enough cash to hire a crew of men to do the digging for him. I wonder if Mama has a recipe for vinegar pie that I could make for everyone to eat at lunch on Wednesday.

# Mama's Vinegar Pie

4 eggs
1½ cups sugar
¼ cup melted butter
1 teaspoon vanilla extract
1½ tablespoons vinegar
9-inch deep-dish pie crust

Mix eggs, sugar, butter, vanilla, and vinegar well. Pour mixture into the crust.

Bake in a medium oven for about 50 minutes until the custard is firm. Let it cool.

Add a topping of whipped sweet cream or meringue if you wish. (It's also tasty served plain.)

There's been frost every night during the past week. Twice we saw a little field mouse run across the kitchen floor. It made Nell scream both times. Those tiny creatures always come indoors, looking for refuge, when the weather turns cold. They're very cute and don't upset me, but they can cause much damage eating food, candles, and whatever else suits their fancy. Last year a mouse even chewed a hole in my bed quilt. Somewhere there's a blue calico nest!

When she saw the second mouse, Mama told Nell to bring one of the barn cats indoors for a couple of days. Unlike the mice, the cats have good coats of fur and don't seem to mind the cold weather. In two days the cat caught six mice. Tim went about the house looking for any small crevices that needed plugging. We sent the cat back outside, but we'll probably see more mice before the winter's over.

Despite the cold nights, when the sun comes up in the morning, the frost quickly melts and the temperature rises. Since the ground hasn't yet frozen, the men can continue digging the new well. Eddie and Cole have come by twice, yesterday and again today. The men take turns climbing down the well hole and handing up pails of dirt. Sometimes it looks as if they are creating a new mountain on our property and not a well.

Usually when they take a rest, Nell and I bring them some biscuits or slices of bread and butter and a cool drink. Then we sit and listen while they talk. I've discovered that Cole has a hundred stories with which to entertain everyone.

He lives in town with his aunt and uncle. I think both of his parents are deceased. Cole's uncle works at the mill, and Cole works there part-time too. But he prefers the outdoor labor of farmwork, and so he hires himself out whenever he can. Last winter when our neighbor, Mr. Adams, broke his leg, Cole went and stayed at his house for three months, sleeping in the kitchen. He helped out with all the chores so well that Mr. Adams took his time getting well. "It was the first and only vacation I ever had," he told everyone.

Among the stories Cole told was one about helping the Adams family with their sheep shearing last spring. He and two other men kept busy catching the sheep and cutting off their thick fleece. The Adams son, Jeff, who isn't thought to be too bright, was told to carry the fleece to the hayloft. One of the workers made a dollar bet with Jeff Adams that they would finish shearing before he would store all the fleece in the hayloft. Well, there were forty sheep in all and the men worked hard and soon had done all the shearing except for one old buck. They looked all over for the sheep but couldn't find it. Eventually they heard him baaing. Jeff had managed to carry the sheep up the ladder to the hayloft.

"Jeff ended the afternoon a dollar richer than he began," said Cole.

"I guess he isn't so dumb after all," my brother Tim said as all of us laughed at the story.

"Seems to me I've heard that same story about someone else," Papa said.

Personally, I can't imagine anyone carrying a big fat old ram up a ladder. Still, it made a fine tale.

The good news is that the men have at last

reached water. Now the new well is already in operation. Unfortunately that means there won't be any reason for Cole to come by this way again. I shall miss his stories. They enliven my day and give me something to relate in my letters to Dossi.

Yesterday afternoon, as I was walking through the yard carrying drinks for the men, I happened to look up at the sky. It was a clear and bright day, but I noticed that the clouds looked like fish scales. We call that a mackerel sky, and it means that the weather is going to change. Perhaps it will finally rain, I thought.

As the afternoon progressed, a wind began to blow and the temperature dropped.

"Will it rain?" Mama asked Papa when he walked into the kitchen.

"Maybe yes, maybe no," he said.

The answer, as it turned out, was no. But before the afternoon was over, the sky grew dark, and large, wet snowflakes began to fall. They landed on the trees, which were still covered with leaves. And by the time we went to sleep, there were six inches of snow on the ground.

The last thing I heard before I went upstairs

to bed was Mama saying, "Early winter."

Some people claim that Vermont has nine months of winter and three months of poor sledding. And others say that our area has only two seasons: winter and the Fourth of July. Both sayings reflect that our winters are long and hard. But this morning when I looked out the window, it was all so beautiful that I didn't worry about the cold months ahead. Besides, for all our complaints about it, snow, like the well, is an excellent source of water. No wonder Papa was smiling as he ate his breakfast.

🌿 Friday, September 29, 1911

Last night as I lay in bed, I could see the moon through the window.

Some people say you can make a wish on a new moon. Others say a full moon is the time for wishing. As I stared at the golden disk in the sky, I found myself thinking of Cole Berry. I wonder if he likes me. I know I find him in my thoughts more and more these days. I don't really believe in the power of the moon to grant wishes. Still, I wished that Cole would think I'm prettier than Josie Wheeler.

This afternoon I suddenly realized that since this journal contains my private thoughts, I must keep it hidden from prying eyes. By that, of course, I mean Nell.

"Why do you write so much?" she asks me. "What are you saying? I want to see." I let her read the first few entries. But now I am beginning to think of this book as a private place to figure out my thoughts, and I don't need my little sister teasing me because I'm sweet on someone. At first I decided that instead of leaving the journal with my undergarments in the chest we share, I would take it up to the hayloft. I knew it would be safe, because Nell is timid of the mice that run about up there. But then I realized that as the weather continues to get colder, my bottle of ink would freeze, making it impossible for me to write there, and it would be too much trouble to carry the ink back and forth. So after some thought, I've decided to hide my journal under the boxes in the little attic storage room next to ours. It's where guests, like Dossi, sleep. But as we have no guests and are expecting none in the months ahead, my book will be safe and private. I hope Nell won't think to look for it there.

Tuesday, October 17, 1911

We woke to more than a foot of fresh snow this morning. Despite the calendar date, winter has really begun.

This time Tim shoveled a path to the barn and another to the woodshed. Nell and I spent a lot of time bringing in armloads of wood for the stove, though I made two trips to every one of hers. We filled the wood box and then brought in still more. If there is another snowstorm, it will be difficult to get outside. So we piled the extra logs neatly against the kitchen wall. We would have been late for school, but since the roads were so covered with snow, most of the students wouldn't have made it. So we too stayed home. It was warm and cozy in the kitchen, and as Mama had two loaves of bread baking, the smell added to my sense of well-being.

In the afternoon, while Nell was outdoors making a snowman, Mama took me aside. She looked very serious, and I worried that I had done something wrong. "Emma," she said, her dark eyes looking concerned. "Will you be very upset if you don't return to school tomorrow?"

"You mean because of the roads?" I asked. "You know they'll be clear by then unless we get another big snowfall tonight."

"Not because of the snow," Mama said. "There's just too much work for Papa and Tim to do on their own now that Eddie isn't living at home. Tim pulled a muscle shoveling the snow this morning. He was able to milk the cows, but he couldn't lift his arm to pull down the hay to feed them. I made a poultice for him. He needs to rest his shoulder for a day or two."

"I should have thought twice before I bought those new cows in the spring," Papa said, coming into the kitchen and warming his hands at the stove. "I knew Eddie wouldn't be here, but the creamery is expanding and was eager to get more milk from us. It was just greed on my part, and now I'm paying for it."

"Ambition is not the same as greed," Mama chided him. "Twenty cows are manageable. And we can use the extra money that you're making. You're just not readjusted yet to winter work. In a few days, you will have set up a new routine. And when the weather is warm again, the cows take care of themselves."

"They can't ever milk themselves," I said. "But I can help. I could milk them before I leave for school. And the evening milking is after Nell and I return home."

"Wait," said Mama. "There's more."

"More cows?" I asked, puzzled.

"More work," said Mama. "There's going to be another baby in our family," she said softly.

"You mean Eddie and Libby's baby?" I asked. "Surely Libby can manage."

"No, no. Another baby. Here," said Mama. "I'm going to have a baby too."

"You?" I asked in amazement. "Aren't you too old?"

Mama smiled. "I thought so. After all, I am

thirty-eight. But apparently these things happen."

"When?"

Mama looked at me, horrified. "When did it happen?" she asked, her face red with embarrassment.

I hugged her. "When is this baby arriving?" I wanted to know.

"The baby is due just about the same time as Eddie and Libby's child," she said. "It will be nice. They can play together."

"Why didn't you say something sooner?" I asked. "The last weeks we've talked about the other baby so much."

"At first I wasn't certain," said Mama. "And then I didn't want to steal Libby's thunder. Libby is as proud as a chicken with two heads. And no wonder. There's something very special about one's first baby." Mama paused a moment and then put her arms around me. "But every child is special. You're my firstborn daughter. Nell's my baby. Or rather, Nell was my baby."

"Nell won't mind giving up her position in the family. She's been very jealous that Eddie's child won't be living here. She thinks it will be a new and better doll to play with."

"She'll soon learn otherwise," said Mama. "But you see, that's why I need you at home. I get tired so easily these days, and I'm often short of breath."

"Of course I'll stay home," I said.

"So you won't mind not going to school?" Papa asked. He had been standing silently as Mama explained the situation. "You've completed eighth grade. You don't really need any more schooling."

"I only had six years," Mama added.

"I know how to read," I said. "I can borrow books from the teacher and from the town library. I can learn what I want," I added. "Literature and history are interesting to me. And I already know more mathematics than I'll ever need. I can add and subtract to keep a budget. I don't need algebra, for heaven's sake."

"I've been teaching you everything you'll need to know for running a household," Mama said. "Nell is a dear, but she's as clumsy as a cow with its foot stuck in the mud. When you were her age, you already knew how to make butter and cheese and could do it as well as me." She paused, smiling, and then went on, "You've learned how to put up extra produce and make jams, you can make bread and pastry, you know how to do plain stitching and fancywork. . . ." She stopped for breath.

"I can roast a chicken and do the laundry, iron the clothes, and clean the house." I laughed.

"And you have a lighter touch with the cows than either of your brothers," added Papa. I'd never heard him say that before! "Someday you'll make a good wife for some lucky fellow," he added.

"She's not getting married so fast," protested Mama. "We'll see. Maybe next year, after the baby is born, you can go back to school," she said.

But the idea of staying home had taken hold. Unlike Nell, who adores school, or Dossi, who writes me long letters about her new high school in New York City, I'm not a scholar. Although I enjoy reading, I take the greatest pleasure from doing things with my hands. I like to be outdoors. I like to plan my own schedule. And the thought of not being locked into a school routine greatly appeals to me. I thought about Uncle Willie. He's not a real relation—he's our neighbor up the road, Wilson Bentley. He never completed a formal education, but he's taught himself loads of things about the weather and nature. Why, he knows more than most scholars, and he's even written articles for national magazines about his study of snowflakes. He's often told us that being self-taught is just as good as being university trained. So I'll read when I want, and knit when I want, and milk the cows when they want. I think it's a wonderful plan. And imagine, two new babies in our family at the same time. It's amazing!

And by the way, amazed is the way Nell took the news of my leaving school.

"Does this mean you're all grown up?" she asked incredulously.

"Of course," I said, feeling suddenly very important.

"Well, you look just the same to me," she said. "I'm glad I'm not going to have to stay home all day. It would be too boring. I always have such fun with my girlfriends at lunchtime. We share our food and we tell jokes and play games."

"I hope that's not all you get out of school," I said to her. "What about studying?"

"I study," Nell said. "I'm already in the advanced math book like some of the older students."

"I know, I know. I was only teasing," I reassured her.

Dossi, too, will be surprised when I write to her about the decision for me to stay home. She told me during her visit that many girls from her elementary school didn't continue with their education. "They're all working in factories now," she said.

I would hate to be cooped up inside a factory building. I'm lucky that my work here will take me outdoors as well as in. Of course, some days in the winter ahead, the outdoor temperature may drop to twenty degrees below zero.

## Thursday, November 2, 1911

Tim has found himself a job, and this is how it happened. Even though Nell and I had trudged the three miles through snow to school, now that Nell is making the journey alone, Mama and Papa began to worry. They wouldn't have sent her off to school if the roads were really bad, but even with the snow cleared off, they worried about icy patches. I know they were thinking about the ankle she broke last winter when she was foolishly showing off while ice-skating. So Tim, whose shoulder has still been bothering him despite the lineament that Mama has been applying twice a day, offered to hitch up our horse, Dandy, to the sleigh and drive her as far as the Thomas sisters' house each morning. That would mean she would have company for the last part of her trip. My parents thought it was a good plan.

The very first morning when they pulled up at the house, Mrs. Thomas came out and said to Tim, "It is so kind of you to drive the girls to school in this freezing weather. I always worry about Jenna and Alyssa."

"How could I tell her that I didn't plan to go any farther?" Tim asked with a grin. So he drove the extra mile.

"Two miles," said Mama. "It was two miles of extra driving, since you had to turn around and come home again."

"One mile, two miles, it's all the same to Dandy," said Tim. It was apparently all the same to him, too. He was glad to be out on the road and not working in the barn. Before he knew it, several other girls were waiting at the Thomases' house, and he was collecting a whole sleighful each morning. And after the first week, Mrs. Thomas put a dollar bill in his hand. "Once is a favor," she told Tim. "Five times a week is a job."

She must have spoken to the parents of the other girls, too, because Tim is collecting five dollars a week now. "I'm going to be rich," he reported, proudly showing off a fistful of bills. "Five dollars a week in twenty weeks is a hundred dollars. And I bet when the snow is gone, the girls won't want to walk in a strong wind or heavy rain."

"What kind of a farmer are you if you don't know not to count your chickens before they are hatched?" Mama asked Tim.

"I'm not much of a farmer," he said. "I'm saving up my money, and you know what I want to buy?" And before any of us could make a guess, he startled us with his answer. "An automobile. A Model T Ford Runabout like Dr. Hascom has."

"An automobile? Really? Oh, will you drive me to school in it?" begged Nell.

"Of course," said Tim. "I'm going to open a livery service. I'll drive people all over: up to Burlington, down to Rutland, wherever."

"You couldn't fit so many girls in one of those Runabouts," Mama pointed out.

"I guess I'll worry about that after I've saved up the six hundred and eighty dollars that it costs," said Tim.

"But if you're driving an automobile all the time, who will milk the cows and help Papa on the farm?" Nell wanted to know.

I knew the answer to that question. But it will take a long time for Tim to earn enough money to purchase one of those automobiles. And by then, perhaps he'll have changed his mind and want to spend his money on something else. But I must confess, a livery service is probably the perfect work for Tim. His passengers would be a ready audience for the stories and jokes he likes to tell. Now that Eddie is gone, his only listeners on the farm are Papa and the livestock. Papa's hearing is bad in one ear, and though Dandy and the cows don't have hearing problems, at least as far as we know, they never respond to Tim's stories at all.

I'm enjoying my freedom from school. These mornings I wake and dress quickly so I can go and help Papa. Getting out of bed on a winter's morning is about the hardest thing in the world. Many mornings it's so cold in our bedroom that I can see my breath when I exhale. I keep my clothing close to my bed and dress while I'm still under the covers. Then I go downstairs and have a swallow or two of hot coffee before I make my way to the barn. The cows are waiting patiently. It's always surprisingly warmer in the barn because of the heat that they give off. In fact, some farmers have constructed their homes with the barns attached so there is a common wall. Then the animal heat from the barn helps to keep the interior of the house warmer. Of course, those homes smell of cows and manure.

There is something quite wonderful about milking a cow. I lean against her body and I pull on her udders. The warm milk streams down into the pail as the cow stands patiently chewing her cud. All of our cows have names: Bettie, Jill, Sukey, Bossy, Jennie, Hettie, Hattie, and the others. We used to have a Libby, but when Eddie announced he and Libby Greene were getting married, Papa said we'd better change the name of our cow. So our cow Libby became Lily, but she still smells like a cow.

After each cow is milked, I pour the pails into the huge milk cans that Papa will take to the creamery. Then I give all the cows fresh hay and clean up around their stalls. By the time I'm finished, I'm almost hungry enough to eat some hay myself. But luckily when I get back to the house, there is always a much better breakfast waiting: hot oatmeal with a dab of golden butter melting into it and newly baked bread, still warm from the oven and spread with homemade blackberry jam. And sometimes as a special treat, Mama makes a batch of pancakes, which we eat with our own maple syrup. Poor cows. They don't know what they miss out on.

৯৫ Tuesday, December 19, 1911

*I*t's a while since I've written because it's so cold up here that I've been putting off sitting down with my journal. But if I really want to keep a record of my days, I have to put on an extra sweater and sit down and write.

Last night after supper, Tim said that the millpond had totally frozen over. "I'm going skating," he announced. "Do you want to come along with me?"

"I'd love to," I responded at once.

"Me too. Me too," Nell called out excitedly.

But Nell had been sneezing all through our meal, and Mama insisted that she stay home. "I'll fix you hot milk with honey," Mama told her.

"All right," Nell agreed, licking her lips in anticipation.

Hot milk with honey is considered a cure and a treat, too, so Nell was distracted and Mama was pleased. Ever since Nell broke her ankle skating last winter, Mama worries about my little sister's well-being.

"Dress warm," said Tim as he wrapped his scarf around his neck.

I put on two sweaters under my jacket and pulled my knit cap down over my ears. It was indeed very cold outside, but there was a full moon lighting our way and casting wonderful shadows as we walked.

Tim says he believes that in the future loads of people will have telephones for communication. But I don't think it's necessary. Without saying a word to anyone, or making any plans or arrangements, there were at least two dozen people already skating when we arrived. The pond is always a popular site during the winter after it freezes.

Someone had built a big bonfire at the water's edge, and it lit the area as well as giving us a place to stop and warm our fingers before we laced up our skates. I looked around, and despite the caps and scarves that hid much of their faces, I recognized just about everyone who was there. Josie Wheeler was gliding along in a bright blue jacket and matching tam with a huge pom-pom. I wished my jacket was more colorful. But looking at her hat made me realize that I could at least knit myself something similar.

I watched her for a moment and thought that her expression was very smug. Since her father owns the mill, which is located on the pond, she acts as if the pond is his, too.

Well, I happen to know that it is community property and doesn't belong to any one person! I pushed off onto the ice, and although I hadn't been on skates since last March, I immediately had my balance and felt the joy of gliding along. Suddenly someone took me by the arm and was skating alongside me. I caught my breath with surprise and turned my head.

"Cole Berry," I scolded. "You might have knocked me down."

"But I didn't," he said, grinning. "Besides, I can see you are a very good skater. You won't knock down so easily."

We crossed arms and skated around the pond without speaking. It was absolutely wonderful, almost as if we were flying. Once someone bumped into us, but Cole held on to me firmly, and though we stumbled, we kept our balance. "Yes," he said. "You're a very good skater."

"Eddie taught me when I was little," I said. As we skated along, I looked for the blue of Josie's jacket. I wanted to see her expression when she noticed my partner. But she seemed to have disappeared.

After our fourth loop around, Cole steered us toward the fire. I was out of breath, but whether it was from skating or the thrill of having such a handsome partner, I can't say. Someone handed me a roasted apple on a stick. It was partly burnt and very hot. But it was delicious and warmed my insides.

"Oh, Cole," a voice called out. I turned and saw that Josie Wheeler was standing nearby. She must have gotten off the ice while we were skating. She stood leaning against a tree and smiled up at him. I once heard Eddie say that, despite her good looks, Josie wasn't very bright.

"Appearances and brains are two different things," I had replied.

"Well," he had said, "she's so stupid that if you put her brain in a bird, it would fly backward."

That made me laugh. Still, I must admit, Josie Wheeler is awfully pretty.

"Can I lean on you?" she asked, giggling at Cole. "I'm afraid that I'm going to fall."

"Can't you skate?" he asked her.

"Not very well. But if you help me, maybe I can manage."

I'd never heard such a brazen lie in my life. Twenty minutes ago Miss Josie Wheeler was whizzing along on the ice. And now suddenly she couldn't skate very well. Who was she fooling? Well, of course, Cole Berry, that's who. And it worked! Maybe she wasn't so stupid after all.

Cole nodded to me and took her by the arm. "Now just relax," I heard him say. "If you hold your body too tensely, you won't be able to get into the rhythm of the movement." I watched as he put his arm protectively around Josie. Suddenly the apple I was eating lost all its taste. I threw it into a mound of snow nearby and looked at them as they moved slowly off across the pond.

I was still looking a moment later when they were both down on the ice with Josie on top of Cole. She had managed to pull him down. Good. Maybe he'd come back and skate with me again. It would be much safer.

But no. Cole jumped to his feet and helped Josie up. Even from where I was I could hear her loud laughter. Cole dusted the snow from her clothes, and they began skating again.

It seemed to me that, just as Josie acts as if the water we were all skating on belongs to her, she also acts as if she has a personal claim to Cole. He is employed by her father. Perhaps that's why he agreed to go off with her so readily, I thought.

"Come, let's skate together," Tim said to me. I was glad to be distracted, and when I smiled at him he said, "You have a piece of burnt apple skin sticking to your teeth."

It bothered me that the last sight Cole had of me last night was with something stuck in my teeth. But at least I didn't make him fall. He's probably all black and blue today. It serves him right. I hope Josie Wheeler is all stiff and sore too. Oh dear. I've become such a mean person, but I can't help it.

## 🌸 Christmas Night, 1911

*L*ast year, and for as long as I can remember, Mama has prepared a large meal for us after church services. This year Libby invited us to dine with her and Eddie. Mama was surprised but pleased. Libby had said several times that she wanted us to come to their house, but this was the first official invitation.

"I bet she's been practicing her cooking all this time," said Nell.

"Don't be foolish," said Mama. But despite her protest, I think she and I agreed for once with Nell. Mama is known to be a fine cook. Libby is not.

We packed the sled with holiday gifts for Libby and Ed, and Mama also brought a pot of vegetable soup and a large mince pie that I had prepared. While we were in church, these items waited in the sled and did not have to listen to the very boring sermon the way the rest of us did. But still, I did not mind sitting in our pew and speculating on the holiday meal ahead. Once at their home, we didn't have long to wait. Even before we entered the door of their house, I could smell something burning. It was a large chicken that had been put into the oven at too high a temperature.

"Sit down," I told my parents. "Let me help Libby while you and Tim talk with Eddie."

"Where are your parents?" I asked Libby. I was surprised that her mother wasn't in the kitchen helping her. It occurred to me that I hadn't seen the Greenes at church, either.

"They're spending Christmas with my aunt in Montpelier. She was widowed this summer, and my parents thought it would cheer her and her children if there was company in the house over the holiday."

I nodded and grabbed an apron that Libby had hanging on the door and put it on over my church dress. Poor Libby look flustered and greasy and badly in need of help. Because she wanted to look her best, she hadn't thought to temporarily cover her clothing until we arrived. As a result, there were grease stains on her shirtwaist. I gave her a kiss and wished her a happy Christmas. "Oh, Emma," she said, practically in tears. "This will be the worst Christmas of my life. Why didn't I just go to eat with your parents? Why did I want to show off?"

"Hush," I told her. "Mama is so pleased not to have to cook today that whatever you serve her will taste delicious. Go put some talcum on those stains while I rescue that poor hen."

So there I was carving the meat off the chicken so that no one need see the burnt skin when another guest arrived. It was Cole Berry!

He walked into the kitchen and greeted me. "You aren't the cook I was expecting to see," he said. Afterward I thought that if he'd passed through the sitting room and discovered my parents and Nell and not me, where did he think I was? But at that moment, I thought only of my flushed face and the hair that had pulled out of its ribbon.

"I'm giving Libby a hand," I told him.

"Two hands," he corrected me. "And four hands are even better. Is there anything I can do to help too?"

My father and brothers would sooner starve than help in the kitchen, so his words took me by surprise. "Do you know how to mash potatoes?" I asked, handing him the masher.

I had already pared off the burnt parts where

the potatoes stuck to the pan when the water had cooked off. Poor Libby had messed up almost every dish she planned to serve. But I knew that with Mama's vegetable soup and the mince pie for dessert, we would not go hungry. I put a large dollop of butter into the bowl of potatoes (sniffing first to be certain that the butter was fresh and not rancid), and I poured an ample amount of milk into the bowl too. I smiled as Cole mashed away. How handy to have his muscles at my service.

Libby had already set the table. There were bowls of bread and butter pickles, applesauce, coleslaw, and a loaf of sliced bread waiting. The china dishes from her trousseau were pretty, white with sprigs of ivy all around. And she had put out two tiny cut-glass vases with real ivy at either end of the table. At least Libby knew how to make the table look attractive, I thought. But of course, one can't eat ivy! I brought in the vegetable soup, which I'd heated and transferred from our big pot to an ornate tureen.

Eddie sat at the head of the table and Libby, clothed now in a different outfit, sat facing him. Her hair was combed, and she looked less flustered. We bowed our heads and said grace. It was only while looking down that I noticed I was still wearing the apron.

Two pregnant women at one table meant that there was talk about babies and cradles. Eddie was busy crafting one now that he couldn't plan on taking the one that he and Tim and Nell and I had once used. Papa gave advice.

Tim, Eddie, and Cole discussed when they would begin cutting the ice that would be stored in icehouses. Every year after the water in the ponds freezes, it is cut in thick blocks and packed with layers of sawdust between the layers of ice. This ice is used to keep our food cool during warm weather.

And then the talk about ice led to talk about ice-skating.

"Emma. You're a fine skater," said Cole, turning to me. "Not like some I could mention. How about coming skating with me tomorrow night?"

"Me too. Me too," called out Nell at once. "I'm a fine skater too. I want to go with you."

"You're a fine skater when you don't break your bones," said Tim, reminding her of last winter's accident.

"I don't know," Mama began.

"Oh, Mama," said Tim. "I'll take the girls and I'll take you, too, if you want to risk it," he said, grinning.

"Certainly not," said Mama. "I'm too old for skating. But I guess if you go along, it's all right."

"Good," said Cole, biting into a slice of the mincemeat pie. "Oh. This is wonderful," he said. "Libby, did you make it?"

Libby blushed and shook her head. "Mama Meade made the soup and the pie," she said. "I hope when I am married as long as she that my food will be as good."

"Do you hear me complaining?" Eddie called across the table to his wife.

"Oh, you come in from the fields so hungry that you'd eat the table if there was nothing on it," said Libby with a giggle. She seemed to have forgotten how upset she'd been when we arrived. And Mama seemed to have forgotten that I made the pie. But I didn't say anything to correct the impression that it was all her work.

There was a large box of chocolates on the table, which was a great treat. It isn't often that we have store-bought candies. It turned out that they had been brought by Cole. I bit into one with a cherry inside, and it dribbled down my chin. I was embarrassed as I wiped the sweet liquid with my napkin and licked my fingers. I looked up and noticed Cole watching me. He gave me a wink, and I felt myself blushing. Luckily everyone was so busy picking out chocolates and talking that I don't think anyone noticed.

When the meal was over, I told Libby to sit still. "Nell and I are very experienced dishwashers," I told her.

Nell made a face at me. She wanted to stay with the adults and listen to their conversation. I did too. But I knew Mama expected us to give Libby a hand. Somehow, just knowing that Cole Berry was in the next room was enough to keep my mood up. And of course, I was already thinking of our ice-skating together tomorrow evening.

※ Tuesday, December 26, 1911, so early that the cows are still sleeping

*I*'m up early because I'm thinking about the ice-skating tonight. Nell is asleep, but I've lit the oil lamp and I'm writing with a quilt over my shoulders to keep me warm. Outside I can hear the wind blowing and the creaking of tree limbs.

Of all the holiday gifts that I received, the most amazing gift was from Papa. He gave me a cow! Really. "You have been working as hard as Tim," he said to me. "Tim receives a portion of the profits to build himself a nest egg for the future. It only seems fair that you should have the same." As a result, Lily (formerly Libby!) is now considered *my* own personal possession. I shall receive one-twentieth of the profits Papa receives from the creamery, and when he is next paid, I will go with him to town and open my own bank account. Papa says that the average income from the milk, cream, and butter of a healthy cow is about seventy-five dollars a year.

"Heavens," I gasped when he told me that. "You will have a very rich daughter!"

"It will be good to have money in the bank for the future," Mama said. "Whether you return to school or marry, money is very important."

"Let's not count our chickens before they are hatched," Papa warned.

"Or our cows," I said, laughing, not that cows can hatch. I was quite stunned by this unexpected gift.

Other presents included a box of new pencils from Tim, a hand-stitched flannel nightgown edged in eyelet lace from Mama, and three hand-kerchiefs from Nell (it is the same gift she has given me for the past three years, but one can see the slight improvement in her embroidery skills from year to year).

Mama gave Eddie and Libby a second full-size quilt that she'd been piecing for them all autumn long. And she'd filled a box with an assortment of jars of food we'd preserved: straw-berry jam, half sour pickles, stewed tomatoes, corn, and beans. Tim carried the box into the house. It was heavy with good fixings to go with future meals. I'd crocheted a sweet little afghan for my unborn niece or nephew, and Nell pre-sented Libby with a pair of handkerchiefs on

69

which she'd embroidered Libby's full initials: *LGM*.

Eddie and Libby apologized for not giving us anything more than Christmas dinner. But Mama was quick to point out that they were giving her the first grandchild. Libby beamed when Mama said that. I wish I had Mama's knack for saying the right thing at the right moment like she does.

One more gift: I received a little package in the mail from Dossi in New York City. She has been so busy with her heavier school load and helping her sister with the new baby that she has written fewer letters to me in recent weeks than she did a year ago. But I treasure each one that arrives. The letters are a gift too, giving me a glimpse of another world and way of life. Dossi is working hard at school with the goal of becoming a doctor in the future. Dossi must have been thinking about my education, or lack of it, when she selected my holiday gift. It is a small, leather-bound volume of a play by Mr. William Shakespeare, *Romeo and Juliet*. The language is strange because it was written so far in the past (more than three hundred years ago, I believe), and it is all in dialogue because it is meant to be performed on a stage. "This is something that my English class has read and discussed," Dossi wrote in a letter accompanying the book. "We've also read *Macbeth* and *Richard III*, all by the same author. My teacher says that anyone who hasn't read these plays cannot consider themselves educated." I don't think Lily or Dandy will care whether or not I'm acquainted with Mr. Shakespeare's work, but I do look forward nevertheless to reading the play. I already wrote thanking Dossi for such a lovely gift. From peeking ahead, I think the story is absurd. It is all about a young man (Romeo) who falls deeply in love with a young girl (Juliet), but because their parents are at odds, they are forbidden to see each other. It is truly melodramatic, though the language, once one gets adjusted to its peculiarities, is actually very beautiful. I begin to see why this play has survived for so long despite the ridiculous story. Unlike my favorite books, such as the novels by Louisa May Alcott and Harriet Beecher Stowe, it's not like real life at all.

Same day, after supper

*T*his turned out to be a day filled with drama! To begin with, after I wrote my morning entry, I turned off the lamp and went back to bed. I fell asleep and was wakened by Nell. She pounced on the bed and shouted, "Look out the window. It's snowing."

"Snowing? Of course it's snowing. This is winter, isn't it?" I retorted. During a Vermont winter, there are very few days when we don't get snow showers. But even before I got to the window, I became aware of the fierce wind outside. When it blew, the window rattled and cold air found its way through the tiniest chinks in the wall. I guessed that the temperature outside was at least twenty below zero. I looked out and saw that this was a true blizzard.

I dressed quickly to go and help with the milking. Early in the fall, Papa had tied a strong, thick rope connecting the house and the barn in preparation for just such a day as this. That way, even if we're blinded by snow, we can always hold onto the rope and not lose our sense of direction.

There are horror stories of farmers who have frozen to death just yards from their homes during blizzards.

We had trouble opening the door because the snow had drifted against it. We could tell that the temperature had dropped drastically during the night. I was right about the extreme cold, because my nostrils froze together when I tried to breathe. And even though I held on to the rope, the wind blowing against me made walking very hard.

Tim and Papa moved ahead, making a path, but it disappeared almost at once from the wind. By the time we reached the barn, we were all freezing cold. I could not feel my fingers or toes. My clothing was covered with snow, and it took a full minute until I could brush most of it off. Papa lit a fire in the old woodstove, and I put my mittens on it to dry them.

I thought of our sleigh ride back from Eddie and Libby's house. What a change in the weather in just a few hours!

"Where did all this snow come from?" I asked Tim accusingly, as if he was the cause. Ordinarily a blizzard doesn't upset me, but today it made me grumpy. I knew it meant that the ice-skating party would be canceled.

"It must have been waiting in the heavens just for you to walk out the door. I didn't see any snow on my way here," Tim replied.

Papa snorted. He knows that Tim likes to josh, but he doesn't approve of lying.

I pulled a pail down from the rack and sat down by Lily to begin milking.

"No skating tonight," said Tim.

My hands automatically continued pulling on Lily's udders. "I think I figured that out already," I said. "How much snow do you think we've gotten so far?" I asked.

"There's at least a foot," said Papa. "But from the intensity of the storm, I guess we can expect double that again."

Tim let out a whistle.

"Darn," I mumbled softly.

"At least Uncle Willie will be happy," Papa said, grinning at us. Our neighbor, Mr. Bentley, is so fascinated by snowflakes that there can never be too much snow for him.

Since I couldn't look forward to an evening of ice-skating ahead, I relived the happy moments of yesterday as I milked the cows. I thought about when Cole and I were working together in the kitchen and when he winked at me across the dining table. I remembered how he complimented my ice-skating. There will be another chance, I told myself. And for once I am glad that winter lasts a long time here in Vermont. There should be many more evenings of ice-skating before the spring thaw sets in and the ice is no longer safe for skating.

After breakfast I completed my other daily chores. Happily much of what I do is centered in the kitchen area, because that is the warmest place in the house. Despite the wind that kept rattling the door, the big woodstove that constantly needs to be fed repaid us by keeping the kitchen at a comfortable temperature. I began making the crust for a dried apple pie for us to have at suppertime.

"Can we make ice cream from snow?" Nell asked as she watched me. There was too much snow for her to go off to school, and she was already feeling restless and bored.

"Ice cream from snow?" I questioned her.

"Yes. It's delicious. I had it at Jenna's house.

75

She showed me how to do it. It's easy."

"I should think that you'd have enough of that white stuff just looking out the window. Why would you want it inside your stomach, too?"

I finished the pie and placed it in the oven. Then I went to the little back room where we store wood and brought in an extra-large arm-load of it. This was going to be a day when we would burn a great deal. Finally, when nothing else needed my attention, I took out my knitting. I'm making a sweater for Tim. But I'm also making myself a tam out of all the odds and ends of wool that we have. Since the skating has been postponed, this new hat will probably be ready by the time we go.

Mama came into the kitchen with a basket full of mending. "Where's Nell?" she asked me.

I looked around and shrugged my shoulders. I couldn't imagine why Nell would want to be in any other room of our house on such a blustery cold day. The wind seemed to be coming through cracks we'd never known existed. But at least the kitchen, with its large woodstove, remained warm.

"I'll go look upstairs," I offered as I removed the pie from the oven. I thought that perhaps Nell had decided to get under the bedcovers and read in the quiet of our bedroom. She wasn't there and had she been, she wouldn't have been able to read. The wind had blown the snow against the window, and it blocked out the bit of daylight that usually came through. The kerosene lamp wasn't lit, either. I hurried back downstairs.

Tim and Papa came in from the barn, where they had finished putting down fresh hay and clearing away the cow manure. Twenty cows make a lot of manure!

Mama told them that she didn't know where Nell was. "Could she have gone outside?" she asked anxiously. All of us turned our eyes to the hook where Nell's jacket should be. It wasn't there.

I remembered Nell's request to make snow ice cream. "I bet she's getting snow for an ice cream recipe she got from Jenna Thomas," I said.

"Oh, Lord," Mama called out.

"You stay here," said Papa at once. "Tim and

I will look for her." But remembering the danger of getting lost in the blizzard, he found some rope. He made a loop and tied it around Tim's wrist. And then he tied the other end to the outside doorknob. Just opening the door seemed to bring the blizzard inside.

"Don't go out," he said to Mama and me. "Boil some water. She'll want a hot drink when she comes back inside."

Mama was glad to have something to do. I sat down with my knitting, but of course I had no desire to continue. If I hadn't been so busy looking at it before, I would have seen Nell when she slipped out. She must have been so quick that I hadn't felt the chill from the open door. Then I remembered how I'd gone to get extra wood for the stove. That must have been when she made her departure.

I sat feeling sick with worry. In weather like this, it would be so easy to get lost and to freeze to death. It seemed like hours till Papa and Tim returned. Their faces were red, and they were covered with snow. Papa's beard and mustache were totally coated with ice. "Give us some hot tea," Papa said, panting. "We'll catch our breath and go out again."

"Oh, my baby. Where is she?" Mama cried out.

"Hush, hush," Papa said. "She's probably just feet away. And we'll find her. Don't worry."

Find her? But in what condition? Would she be alive or . . . ? Those were the questions that we all left unsaid. "Let me have a turn," I insisted, jumping up. I couldn't sit still. I had to do something. I wrapped my scarf around my neck and face and put on my jacket and hat as I spoke. "Give me the rope," I told Tim.

"No, no!" Mama cried out. "I can't lose both my girls."

"I have no intention of getting lost. But I probably have a better idea about where Nell might have gone. After all, we've played a hundred games around the house." My words sounded confident, but that wasn't how I felt. Still, with the rope around my wrist, I knew Papa and Tim would always manage to find *me*. The question was, could I find Nell?

Outside the wind was even fiercer than it had been when I'd gone to milk the cows. My eyes couldn't see far, and they even had trouble staying open when instinct made me want to shut them tight. My nostrils froze shut and prevented me from breathing. But I breathed through my mouth. I realized that if Papa and Tim had tried shouting or whistling to her, Nell would never have heard them over the howls of the wind. Nor would they have heard her if she had cried for help. I stood in front of the house for a moment and tried to think like Nell. The wind was blowing at my face, so I assumed she'd turn her back on it. I turned around and moved with great difficulty. There was much more than a foot of snow now. There were no tracks, not even from Papa and Tim. The wind kept blowing the snow and changing the landscape. I stood facing our house, but I couldn't even recognize where I was. Just a few yards from the entrance to our house is a large yew bush. Sometimes when she was little, Nell hid underneath its branches as if she was in a cave. The problem was that the drifts of snow were so high, I could not tell what was shrubbery and what was snow.

Inside my gloves my fingers felt numb. I stumbled forward and tripped, landing facedown in the snow. I stayed down for a moment, breathing heavily. I know we've had blizzards before, and as a Vermonter I can look forward to hundreds more. But somehow at that moment I felt colder and more scared than ever before. I hardly had the energy to get up. But I scrabbled with my hands to find support and, miraculously, I realized that I was actually grabbing onto the yew bush. I pushed my way inside. "Nell. Nell," I shouted, praying that she was there.

"Emma?" said a faint voice from within.

No music ever sounded more beautiful than my sister's voice at that moment.

"What in the world are you doing?" I asked Nell, who was hiding deep within the bush.

"I'm pretending that I'm an Eskimo. We were studying about them in geography. And you've come into my igloo. Isn't it cozy?"

"If you stay much longer, you won't be an Eskimo. You'll be a frozen block of ice," I yelled at her. But amazingly, within the bush and out of the wind, we were protected, and it wasn't nearly as cold as outside of it.

I held out my arm with the rope attached and told Nell to grab tightly onto me. "Mama and Papa and Tim are very worried," I scolded.

Out of the bush's protection, we couldn't speak. The wind tried hard to keep us from our door, but we made it just as it opened and Papa and Tim appeared. They grabbed at the rope and pulled us both inside.

"Oh, thank the Lord. She's safe. They're both safe," Mama called out.

"I was playing Eskimo," exclaimed Nell when she caught her breath. "It was lots of fun."

"It was foolish," I said, still gasping.

"It's over. All's well," said Papa, helping Nell remove her frozen jacket. And ten minutes later, we sat around the table together drinking strong hot tea with honey and eating slices of my apple pie.

"Oh, dear," Nell cried out.

"What's wrong?" asked Mama, grabbing Nell's hands. She'd already checked for signs of frostbite, but she worried that perhaps she had missed something.

"I left the pail of snow outside," Nell complained.

"What pail of snow?" asked Tim. "You left the world of snow outside!"

"I went out to get snow to make ice cream. It

would taste so good on this pie."

"I think you had enough snow for one day," said Mama.

The snow and winds continued all day long. Every window became coated with snow, and there were huge, huge drifts. From time to time, Tim or Papa went out and shoveled the snow away from the door. If it froze to the door, we would have to jump out of the windows to get outside. On one of his trips, Tim took a clean milk pail with him. He returned with it filled with clean snow for Nell. Mama was so happy to have Nell safe at home that she readily agreed to let her make the ice cream from snow that she'd sampled at her friend's house.

# Nell's Ice Cream from Snow

1 cup milk
$\frac{1}{2}$ cup sugar
$\frac{1}{2}$ teaspoon vanilla
4 or 5 cups clean snow

Mix together the milk, sugar, and vanilla until the sugar is all dissolved. Add the snow gradually to the sweetened milk. Stir constantly until it is as thick as ice cream. Eat at once!

❧ Friday, January 5, 1912

The blizzard is behind us. Yesterday evening Tim, Nell, and I took our skates and trudged to the pond. Most of the way we could walk on the road, where the snow is packed down from wagon and horses' travel over the past days. The snow was packed and hard on the ground and squeaked under our feet. The sound made me want to laugh.

At the pond there was a large group and a bonfire, just like last time.

Nell sat down on a rock and immediately tied her blades onto her heavy shoes.

"Go carefully," I warned her.

85

"I know, I know," she said with irritation. She knows we'll never let her forget last year's accident.

I found another rock and sat on it myself. I was in the midst of pulling the straps on my right foot tightly when someone pulled my new tam off my head. "I've never seen this hat before," said a voice. "But I do believe I recognize the head."

I looked up with a smile. It was Cole Berry.

Although he was already wearing his skates, he sat down beside me. "Shall I give a strong pull for you?" he offered. And then he took the skate straps in his hands and tied them to my boots.

"Cole! Cole!" a voice called him. "I've been looking all over for you. I need you to help me, like last time."

I looked up and saw Josephine Wheeler standing beside us. A green cap was perched on her blond hair, and her cheeks were red and glowing. There is no question that she is very pretty. Much prettier than I am.

"Why, hello, Josie," Cole responded, standing up.

She grabbed his hand. "Come on, let's skate," she said to him.

Cole looked at me.

I didn't know if I was expected to say something. Should I have told him to go ahead? I didn't want him to skate with Josie Wheeler. But it wasn't for me to decide. Besides, hadn't he invited me to come skating with him?

Cole turned to Josie and smiled. "Josie, you need to practice gliding by yourself," he instructed her. "When we skated together, we kept falling down. I don't want to be the cause of your spills," he said.

He held out his arm to me and I got up.

"Are you going to skate with Emma?" she asked in amazement. She knew she was prettier than me and she couldn't believe her eyes.

"It looks that way," said Cole.

And with that the two of us went off toward the ice.

Now here's the strange thing that happened. Later in the evening, when all our fingers and toes were frozen, I took off my skates and then my boots and rubbed my feet to get the circulation moving. Then a few minutes later, when I turned to put the boots back on, they were missing, although my skates were right where I'd left them. I couldn't walk on the icy ground, so Nell and Tim and Cole looked around for me. I knew I'd left them by the rock. Without getting up from the rock where I was sitting, I looked under shrubbery and near the bonfire.

"If we can't find your boots, I'll carry you back home," Cole called out in a very loud voice.

Amazingly, a few moments later the boots reappeared, just where I'd remembered leaving them.

"This is so strange," said Nell as she watched me putting the boots back on.

"Yes, it is, isn't it," I said. I looked at Cole and he gave me one of his famous winks. Neither of us said a word, but I had a strong suspicion about who might have hidden my boots. I don't know if Cole had the same thought, but I suspect that he did. Of course, in a way I was sorry that the boots were found. I would have enjoyed having Cole carry me all the way home.

*I*'ve always said that Nell speaks too much. The morning after our ice-skating, she prattled on and on about how I'd skated with Cole Berry and how he'd held my hand and spun me around on the ice.

"Didn't you skate with your sister at all?" Mama asked me.

"Why, no," I said, surprised by her question. "I don't usually skate with Nell. She skates with her friends and I skate with mine."

"I skated with Nell for a few minutes," Tim said. "But when she saw Jenna and Alyssa, she up and left me like an old shoe." He pretended he was sad.

"Jenna and Alyssa and I watched Emma and Cole," Nell said. "I hope when I'm as old as Emma, a man will skate with me."

"No one will skate with you if you keep your mouth running on so much," I complained.

Mama handed Nell a bowl of oatmeal. I hoped that would keep her mouth busy. But no. A moment later, after swallowing her first spoonful, she said, "Cole is very handsome. He's more handsome than you," she told Tim.

"Now I really feel like an old shoe," my brother complained.

"That's enough talk about Cole Berry," said Papa, scraping up the last of the cereal from his bowl. "Emma, you're too young to let anyone court you," he added.

"Who said anything about courting?" I asked. "I went ice-skating. Cole went ice-skating, and we skated together."

"Is he courting you?" asked Nell. "I guessed it."

It was too much. I held my tongue, but I thought nothing good could come of all this talk. Papa was sure to get anxious if he thought Cole was sweet on me.

Well, I was right, and it was much worse than I even imagined. Still, I enjoyed my memories as I wrote in my journal that afternoon.

In the evening, as I stood weeping from the onions I was chopping for the next day's stew, there was a knock on our door. We all turned to face the door, as it's very unusual to get visitors in the dead of winter. It was Cole! With a big smile on his face, he handed Papa a gallon jug of cider that he said was a gift. Then he pulled a paper bag from his pocket and showed us cinnamon sticks inside. "I thought on a cold night like this you might want to drink some mulled cider," he said.

After that, it was only common hospitality to invite him inside to share some of the cider with us. Quickly I splashed water on my eyes and washed the smell of onions from my hands. I was afraid that I was red-eyed from all the crying I always do when I cut up onions. Luckily there wasn't a mirror around, so I didn't know how terrible I surely looked.

"That's a heavy jug to carry uphill," commented Tim.

"Well, it's pretty windy outside," said Cole. "So it gave me ballast and kept me from blowing away."

Nell laughed aloud. "I never heard of a person flying away in the wind," she said.

Mama poured the cider from the jug into a large pan and put it on the stove. Then I got out some cloves and allspice and tied them into a little bag made of cheesecloth. I dropped the bag of spices and the cinnamon sticks into the pan of heating apple cider. Mulled cider is very tasty, and I was pleased to think of sharing a cup of it with Cole.

While I was at the stove, Cole sat down with Nell. "Do you know how to play dots?" he asked her.

"Of course," she replied.

"Well, I bet I can beat you," he said. The next thing I knew, Nell was making dots across a piece of paper in both directions and then she drew the first line.

I watched with pleasure. There was something so easy and comfortable in Cole's manner. He was entertaining Nell, and in a few minutes when we all sat around the table, he'd probably amuse the rest of us with his stories of village life. It was as if we'd all known him forever.

Within seconds Nell was laughing and cheering as first she and then Cole connected the lines to make boxes. When they counted them up, Nell let out a whoop. "I won. I won," she said. "I knew I would."

I poured the mulled cider into our mugs and brought them to the table. Papa, Mama, Tim, Nell, Cole, and I sat around the table.

"I hear you were ice-skating with my daughter," Papa said to Cole.

I blushed at the memory.

"Yes indeed, sir," said Cole. "She's an excellent skater."

"She's also an excellent daughter," said Papa. "And I know she'll listen to me when I tell her that she's too young for courting."

"Yes, sir," said Cole, his face turning red as he agreed much too readily for my taste with Papa's words.

"By that I mean, you can greet her when you meet. But you're not to look out for her. No skating together, no walking together. She's only fifteen," said Papa.

"Sixteen in two months," I blurted out.

"Sixteen is still too young for courting," said Papa at once.

"My mother was married at sixteen," said Cole quietly.

"Yes. And where is she now?" asked Mama.

"She's dead. But that has nothing to do with getting married at sixteen," said Cole.

"I'm sorry. I forgot," Mama said to Cole, blushing at her gaffe. "But her father and I don't approve of our Emma getting married at sixteen or seventeen or—"

"My mother died at the age of thirty-four during childbirth when I was born," Cole said softly, ignoring what my mother said about me. "My father always said they'd had a good marriage, even though they were disappointed to be childless for so many years."

Nell interrupted before anything more could be said. "Did Cole ask Emma to marry him?" she asked. For once she'd been sitting quietly because she was so amazed by all the words that were being said.

"No," said Cole before anyone could answer for him. "I just brought some cider to some neighbors. I'm sorry if my presence upsets you, sir," he said to Papa. He pushed his chair away from the table and stood up.

Papa stood too. "No indeed, Cole. You're a fine young man. But you're too old for my daughter. How old are you, anyhow?"

"Nineteen, sir," he said.

"Just like Eddie," said Nell.

"Hush, Nell. No one is talking to you," said Mama.

"I think you'll find a choice of attractive young women closer to your age here in Jericho," said Papa. "I advise you to look in their direction."

My face, which had been blushing all during the conversation, got redder still. I could hardly bring myself to look at Cole for fear that I'd start crying. Cole shook hands with Papa and said good-bye. He left the house without even a glance in my direction. I may never see him again, or at least not at such close range. The next time I see him he'll probably be skating or walking with some other girl, like Miss Josie Wheeler. She's seventeen, and I'm sure her papa will have no objections if anyone comes a-courting.

Mama told Nell it was time for bed. Tim said he was going to check on the cows. We never check on the cows after the evening milking time, but I know he wanted to give me a little privacy, and for that I was grateful. I turned to Papa.

"How could you be so rude to Cole Berry?" I asked him. "You practically threw him out of the house. And he brought us cider, too."

"He brought a courting gift to our family, and

as I've said before, you're too young to be court-ing."

"I'm not too young," I said angrily. "I'm old enough to stop going to school. I'm old enough to do all the chores of an adult. But you're treating me like a child."

"Emma," Mama scolded me. "You should apologize to your father. He's only looking out for your welfare. No good can come of an early marriage. You'd be an old woman before you were twenty. And how could Cole support you? He doesn't own any land. He does odd jobs for whoever needs help."

"You embarrassed me," I shouted. "I didn't hear any marriage proposal. And even if he was thinking of it, I'll never hear it now. You sent him off, and without even asking me how I felt about things."

"I don't care how you feel. Not now. Not when you're still fifteen," said Papa, still holding his mug of cider. At that moment I wished he'd choke on it! That's how angry I felt.

"And next month?" I demanded of him. "Or next year? When will you care how I feel?"

I turned and went upstairs. It was the first

evening since I learned to speak that I went to bed without bidding my parents a good night and pleasant dreams. I hoped that Nell was asleep, for I couldn't imagine saying a single civil word to her, either.

I got into bed, and even though I was far from the kitchen and the onions I'd been chopping when Cole arrived at our house, within moments my pillow was wet with tears.

The next morning Cole's disastrous visit filled my thoughts, and I was crosser than a bear with a sore head. I went to the barn and milked the cows as usual. I had slept badly, thinking of the events of the evening. Would I ever see Cole again? I wondered over and over.

When I saw Papa, I looked him in the eye and apologized for my words the night before. "I'm sorry I lost my temper," I told him, "but I meant everything I said."

"I understand," said Papa. "But I also understand that you are still fifteen years old."

Papa was not going to change his mind and neither was I. So instead of arguing, I kept busy with the milking and cleaning out the cows' stalls. After breakfast, instead of doing needlework or helping in the kitchen with Mama, I kept busy doing other chores. I rechecked the chicken coop for eggs, though there never are many during the winter months. I put fresh straw in the coop and sprinkled extra dried corn for the hens. I cleaned out the woodstove and carried the ashes outside. Then I worked at cleaning the kerosene lamps, trimming the wicks, and filling them with the oil. I brought in many armloads of wood, more than I'd usually lug in one morning. It felt good to drop each load on the kitchen floor with a crash. If I couldn't scream out my anger, at least I could still make a loud noise. And finally when there was no more space to pile up wood, I went down to the cellar and rearranged the jars of pre-served food on the shelves. Usually I take as much pleasure as Mama in seeing all the colorful jars displayed: the reds of beets, strawberries, raspberries, and tomatoes; the different shades of green from beans, peas, and pickles; and the yellow and orange from corn and carrots. The jars represent hard work and good meals ahead. But this time there was no satisfaction in seeing that colorful selection of jars.

Only a letter from Dossi that was delivered later in the day proved to be a temporary distraction. I will write to her and tell her my side of the story, I thought at once. She doesn't have a boyfriend and never writes about caring for anyone, but I know she'll understand how I feel. And it's good that I have this journal to write in, for I think I should explode with my emotions if I couldn't express myself somehow. I want to speak with Cole and find out if he is really interested in courting me. But barring that, I'm glad I can speak on this page.

*January 10, 1912*

*Dear Dossi,*

*It's hard to believe, but suddenly the little book of* Romeo and Juliet *that you sent me for Christmas has turned into the story of my life.*

*I've mentioned Cole Berry in some of my recent letters. I really enjoy his company. But a few nights ago my father forbade him to court me. All we've done is ice-skate together a couple of times. Now I feel so confused and angry. Unlike Juliet, I don't even know how deeply I feel about Cole. But I would like to leave that possibility open and also have a chance to know him better.*

*This afternoon, when my father wasn't around, my mother admitted that Papa had spoken overly harsh the evening when Cole was here. She knows that I know she was only seventeen when she married Papa.*

*"Your father wants you to have opportunities that I didn't," she said, defending him. "Perhaps you'll want to go back to school."*

*I don't. And I know what I can and should do now. I'm not accustomed to disagreeing with Papa. But if I can't see Cole anymore, I know I shall be miserable.*

*Have you ever felt strongly about any of the young men you meet at school or in your neighborhood? You never have mentioned it, but perhaps you are keeping your feelings secret. I wish you were here to discuss this with me. I can't talk to Nell—she's just a baby. And my mother feels she must defend my father's position. For the first time in my life, I feel so alone.*

*Your friend,*
*Emma*

I don't know why, but the very act of writing to Dossi makes me feel a little (but only a little) better. I won't mail the letter yet. I'm leaving it here in my journal.

## Monday, January 15, 1912

*I* was pleased yesterday morning when we woke to clear skies. It meant that we could go to church. I haven't become extra religious because of my dilemma, but it occurred to me that even if we can't speak together, there is a good possibility that Cole will be at the Sunday services.

I dressed with care, combing my hair back from my face and wearing a lace collar that once belonged to my grandmother.

"You look very pretty today," Mama said as we left the house. I wondered if she could read my mind.

We sat in our usual pew on the left-hand side of the church, back four rows. The problem with sitting so close is that you can't observe who is in the back. But I hoped that even if I couldn't see him, Cole was situated somewhere where he could view me.

When we stood to sing a hymn, I tried to unobtrusively turn slightly to see those behind us. Mama smiled at me. I didn't know if she realized what I was trying to do. It made me blush.

I'm not accustomed to trying to deceive my parents.

As the service drew to a close, the minister made an announcement. "Our fine organ player, Mr. Chase, has come up with a wonderful plan. He wants to establish a choir from the members of our congregation."

We all looked at one another with surprise. Mr. Chase has been with us only a few months, and obviously he has big ambitions for our small church.

"Those interested should plan to come to the church at four P.M. on Tuesday," the minister said. "Mr. Chase says he needs all voices, men and women. There will be no auditions. Everyone interested is encouraged to participate."

I enjoy music. Sometimes Mr. Bentley invites us to his home and plays his pianoforte. Then we all sing. A choir might be a good diversion. It suddenly crossed my mind that perhaps Cole Berry likes to sing too. If the weather remains good, I will be in the church promptly at four on Tuesday. And then I will see who the singers are in our church community.

**᠅ Thursday, February 15, 1912**

*I*'ve now gone to three singing sessions at the church. Nell came with me to the first. However, as we sang only scales and no real music during the first half hour, she became restless. She went off with the Thomas sisters to play outside, but I remained singing the scales. The scales helped Mr. Chase plan where we should sit. He told me that I sing soprano, which means that I can get some of the higher notes. Libby, who had also come for the singing, sat a distance away with the deeper female voices that are called alto. The few men who joined us were divided into tenors and bass.

Very few men attended, and Cole was not among them. I would have given up on the idea of the chorus had not Mr. Chase stopped blowing on his pitch pipe and concluded the scales. He handed out some books of music. "You'll have to share them. I don't have enough for everyone today," he said. "But I have ordered more, and they will be here soon." Then he sat down at the organ and played a piece of real music.

"We are going to attempt to study an oratorio by Joseph Haydn," he explained when he stopped playing. "It's called *The Creation*, and the text is taken from the Bible." Of course, we'd all read that on the cover of the books we were holding. But as I can't read music, I had no idea how exciting it would sound. Mr. Chase began singing, "In the beginning God created the Heav'n and the Earth. . . ."

He taught us to sing the first chorus from the oratorio. And when the eighteen people in the room sang their parts, "And the Spirit of God mov'd upon the face of the waters: and God said, Let there be light: and there was light," I actually got gooseflesh.

So even without Cole, I decided that I would

go to the next music session at the church. At least it would be one thing to look forward to during these long, dreary winter days. And here's the wonderful thing. The following week Nell stayed home, and Cole came to the rehearsal.

Now we have a total of twenty-six members of our chorus. Cole sits across the room from me. He is singing in the tenor section. We don't speak together, but whenever I look in his direction, I notice he is looking at me. And when we sing, I imagine I am singing to him and he is singing to me. Once, as we sat listening to instructions from Mr. Chase, I remembered the visitor at the church pie social last fall (she is Mrs. Coolidge—I looked back in this book and found her name). If only Cole and I knew the language of hand signs that Mrs. Coolidge taught her deaf students, we could converse together despite the injunction from Papa. Would it be so dishonest for us to move our fingers as we sit across the room from each other? As it is now, we don't communicate at all. And Cole has so much integrity, remembering Papa forbidding him to speak with me, that he doesn't even give me one of his winks.

In any event, I remember the New England proverb Take what you get and be thankful for that. Even if we don't speak, I can look forward to seeing Cole's handsome face once a week at the choral rehearsal! Unless, of course, the weather cancels the choir, as it has done twice already.

Of course, There's always a sour apple in the barrel. I know I'm not the only one looking at Cole's face. Next to me, another soprano has her eye on him. It's Josie Wheeler. She and her younger sister, Mary, are both in the chorus. Mary has a lovely voice, and Mr. Chase has even promised her a solo part when we perform for the congregation in the late spring. Josie's voice is no better than mine and perhaps is less good, though I admit that I may not be judging her fairly.

Last Tuesday Josie leaned over to me and whispered, "Have you noticed how Cole Berry is always looking at me?"

I flushed red and thought, I certainly haven't noticed that at all.

"Are you sure?" I found myself asking her.

"Just watch him and you'll see," she said, smiling broadly.

Mr. Chase tapped the music stand with his baton. "Ladies, please, no talking. We are here to sing and not to gossip."

I looked across at Cole and thought I saw a flicker of a smile on his face. But was he smiling at me or at Josie? We were sitting so close together that I couldn't figure out the angle of his eyes.

When the rehearsal was concluded, Josie ran to crook her arm through Cole's and they left the church meeting hall together. It doesn't appear to me as if he invites her constant presence, but there it is. Can it be that all this time I thought he was looking at me and he was admiring her?

Yesterday, as the rehearsal ended, I felt someone thrust something into my hand. It was Libby. "This has your name on it," she said.

It was an envelope with my name, but I could not recognize the handwriting. Puzzled, I opened it and pulled out a Valentine card. There was no signature.

"Where did you get this?" I asked her as I pushed the card quickly back inside the envelope.

"It was stuck inside my music book," she said.

I put the envelope inside my pocket and didn't look at it again until bedtime. All the evening, during milking, supper, cleanup, and while I sat knitting, I felt as if there was a live coal burning inside my pocket. But unlike a real coal, this one left no clue of its existence for others to see. Only I knew it was there.

When I finally had a quiet, private moment to remove the card from its envelope again and study it, I could find no mark on it. Who left it for me remains a mystery. There are eleven men in the chorus. Seven are married, two are old widowers, and one is Jack Harvey, who everyone knows is sweet on Mary Wheeler. That means that unless one of those old widowers has an eye on me, the card can only be from one person. Even unsigned, it lifts my heart. I trace my fingers over the slightly raised letters *To My Valentine*. I love knowing that his fingers once touched this card. I will keep it pressed inside this journal and treasure it. It is a secret that I shall share with no one. But then just as I was falling asleep, I had a horrible thought: Could he have given *her* a Valentine too?

Tuesday, February 20, 1912

*T*oday was the weekly choir rehearsal. I look forward to it so much. But my joy was disturbed greatly by Josephine Wheeler. Before the singing, when people were still finding their seats and turning the pages of the music books, she leaned toward me and announced proudly, "My father has offered Cole Berry a full-time job at the mill come spring."

"Oh," I said. I knew Cole already worked for Mr. Wheeler a couple of days a week.

"Yes," said Josie. "I urged Papa to hire him. And if Cole plays his cards right, he might have more than a full-time job." Here she smiled coyly and glanced around to see if anyone was listening. "If Cole married me, I'm sure my father would take him on as a partner."

I caught my breath. "Is that the plan?" I asked, trying to seem unconcerned.

"It is a good plan, don't you think?"

"I guess it's up to Cole Berry to decide if that's what he wants," I retorted.

"Why shouldn't he want it? Didn't your

brother marry Libby Greene so he'd get that piece of farmland from her father?"

"What a dreadful thing to say," I gasped. "Eddie and Libby were sweethearts since they were schoolchildren. It was long before Mr. Greene even bought that extra section of land."

"Perhaps," said Josie, looking as if she knew better.

I might have argued with her more, but Mr. Chase began tapping on his music stand with his baton. "Ladies, ladies," he called to Josie and me. "I need your attention here, please."

The music practice began. I guess I must have sung with everyone else, but I can't recall a single verse or melody. My head was so filled with the hateful thing that Josie had said about Eddie, as if his marriage was based on a scheme to gain land and not because he loved Libby. And of course, I was thinking about how she was trying to bribe Cole into marriage. Well, if he could be bought, he wasn't the person I thought he was. I told myself it was none of my business. Cole was just an acquaintance, and if he married Josie Wheeler that was his affair. But I feel terrible. Who could blame him if he marries Josie? He can't even talk to me.

❧ Sunday, March 3, 1912

*T*oday, instead of attending church, I went off with a basket of goodies for Libby and Eddie. "Just like Little Red Riding Hood," Mama said as she waved good-bye. Of course, I don't have a red hood. Instead, I was wearing my tam and matching scarf. Libby's had a cold for ages, and when I suggested to Mama that I go and visit her, she thought it was a good plan. Yesterday I'd made a huge venison stew with some of the meat from a deer that Tim killed in the fall, and I took a goodly portion of it to my sister-in-law. In addition, I brought a dozen of the ginger cookies that I'd baked. They are very good with a cup of hot tea.

I hadn't seen Libby since the choral rehearsal when she delivered the Valentine card to me because her cold has dragged on for so long. Instead, we'd just hear about her from Eddie: once when I accidentally met him in town when we were both doing errands, and another time when he came out to our house to drop off the jigsaw he'd borrowed from Papa. So when Libby opened the door, I was momentarily startled by her appearance.

"You look as if the baby was due today!" I gasped. Although she's expecting close in time to Mama, she seems to have grown much bigger in the last three weeks. "Do you think you could be having twins?" I asked. That would certainly be an exciting development, even if it meant a lot of extra work for Libby.

"Twins or one big fat baby," said Libby, blowing her red nose.

I removed my coat and went at once into the kitchen, with Libby following behind. "Now you just sit and talk to me," I said. "Tell me all the gossip. And I'll put this stew on the stove to heat up."

"Good gossip is as tasty to chew over as any

meal," said Libby, laughing. "But maybe not as good as the food Mama Meade has sent here."

I stirred the carrots and potatoes that were in the stew gravy and didn't bother to correct Libby. Already the aroma from the stew was filling the air, and she'd given me a compliment even if she didn't know it.

"The big news is that Mary Wheeler accepted a ring from Jack Harvey two days ago. I hear that they will be married in August."

"I'm not surprised," I replied. "We've seen them together at the choral rehearsals. Of course they can't sit alongside each other during the singing, but you just know if Jack could make his voice sing as high as Mary's, he'd be right beside her. They look very happy."

"I'll tell you who's not happy," said Libby, lowering her voice even though there was no one else present to overhear us.

"Who?" I asked, already guessing the answer.

"Josie is hopping mad. She's a year older than her sister and always assumed she would marry first. In fact, she even told some of her friends that August is a long way off, and she just might take the marriage vows before Mary."

"And who would she marry?" I asked, holding my breath, though of course I knew the answer.

"I think it will be anyone she can snare," Libby said with a laugh. "But I know she has her eye on Cole Berry. Now that he's working more hours at the mill, Eddie tells me that whenever he goes by the mill, he sees her hanging around Cole. It's a wonder Cole can do any work for Mr. Wheeler."

I didn't tell Libby about Josie's scheme, arranging with her father to hire Cole full-time when the spring arrived, and how she thought he'd marry her so that he could become part owner of the sawmill. I also didn't mention what Josie had said about my brother marrying her to gain possession of her father's land. That was so certainly a downright lie that I wouldn't repeat it.

Instead, I said, "Do you think Cole Berry has an eye on Josie?" I kept looking at the pot of stew and felt my face turning red from the heat of the stove.

"Cole Berry is too much a gentleman not to greet her at the mill or to turn her down when she invites him to visit at her house or to take her ice-skating," said Libby. "But I believe he's not so enamored of Josie. She has beautiful features, but remember, Pretty is as pretty does. You may never have heard her, but Josie Wheeler has a wicked temper. She ordered a particular shade of blue thread at the general store, and I was there when the thread arrived and she discovered that it didn't match the dress she was making. What a scene she made!"

"Perhaps Cole has never seen her when she displays her temper," I said.

"He's seen her all right," said Libby, blowing her nose again. "He was in the store that day too. And besides, that wasn't the first time she had a tantrum in the middle of town for everyone to see. She flared up when Josh Merryman's wagon splattered her with mud last spring, and she screamed like a madwoman when little Lucy Cox was chasing a ball and ran into her."

"Poor Josie," I said. "She does seem to have things to vex her. I wouldn't like to be splattered with mud either." I was trying to sound generous about Miss Josephine Wheeler, but inside I was wondering how Cole really felt about her.

"Of course not," Libby agreed. "No one wants to have their clothing soiled, but I know you pretty well, Emma Meade. You'd just laugh and go home and clean yourself up. You wouldn't scream at Josh the way she did. Poor Josh with his bright red hair and fair complexion. Believe me, his face matched his hair that day. And the redder he got, the more she yelled, and the more she yelled, the redder he got."

I laughed at the image of poor Josh.

"Everyone loves the honey of the bee, but no one wants to be stung," said Libby.

Just then we heard the door open. "We almost had another guest for dinner," Eddie's voice called out to us as he embraced first his wife and then me. "I saw Cole and invited him to join us. At first he accepted, but when I mentioned that Emma was going to be here too, he excused himself."

"What ever for?" asked Libby. "There's plenty of food."

"Hmmm. And it smells wonderful," said Eddie, sniffing loudly.

I didn't say anything at all. Obviously, Papa's words to Cole have been a well-kept secret that Libby, and I guess Eddie, too, know nothing about. But the thought that Cole had been so near and almost sitting across from me at the dinner table spoiled the taste of my stew. Not so for Libby and Eddie. They scraped their plates and had second helpings.

"There's still some left in the pot," said Libby. "I'll save it in case Cole should come by this evening as he sometimes does. He may not be able to resist Mama Meade's venison stew after all."

"It wasn't Mama who made it," I blurted out this time. "You can tell Cole that I was the one who fixed it." And then, realizing how strange this must sound to Libby and Eddie, I quickly added, "And don't forget to tell him that Tim shot the deer with a single bullet. Everyone should get credit for their efforts."

"And who made the cookies?" asked Libby, biting into one.

"I did," I admitted.

"Isn't she clever?" said Eddie. "These are almost as good as yours," he told his wife.

I've tasted Libby's cookies. My brother is a very gallant husband.

He drove me home before it got dark. I wonder if Cole ate the remaining stew. And I wonder if Libby told him who prepared it.

The days are suddenly warm, and that means it's time to tap our maple trees. Papa, Tim, and I put out the buckets and empty the sap from them regularly. We've begun boiling it down to syrup. It's always a lot of hard, hot work. But I know I won't complain when I'm pouring our own syrup on freshly made pancakes.

I heard from Libby that the Wheelers had a big sugaring-off party. It was a way to celebrate Mary's engagement as well as enjoy the first syrup of the season. I can guess that Cole was one of the guests too.

Some years we have a sugaring party too. In the past I enjoyed the company of our neighbors, the Bentley family and all their children. This year, however, Mama feels too tired for parties. And though the syrup is as sweet as ever, I'm not interested in organizing a party of any sort—not if I can't invite whoever I want. The syrup may be sweet, but it can't sweeten my mood.

$S$uddenly mud season is here. The spring thaw has arrived very early this year. My birthday was on the twentieth, together with the first official day of spring. Usually we look at the calendar in the kitchen and the snow out the window and laugh. But this year the sun was out and the temperature rose to sixty degrees.

"You warm our hearts as the sun warms the earth," Mama said as she kissed me at breakfast time. She was short of breath. I was only six when Nell was born, and I don't remember how Mama was then. I think this pregnancy has taken more energy from her as well as a back tooth. "They say you lose a tooth for every child you bear," Mama told me. But then she said, "Considering I've had seven pregnancies, I've been very lucky. I've only lost three teeth in all."

Lucky? How could she say that when she's lost two babies, both boys, one born before and one after me? I was only eighteen months old when this second infant brother died, and so I have no memory of little Thomas at all.

Mama had made cinnamon rolls for my birthday breakfast, and there were three packages waiting for me: a new notebook, since this one is almost filled up, and a lovely moss-green cardigan sweater all knit in seed stitch and with pewter buttons that Mama has been working on secretly.

"I'm always here," I said. "When could you find time to knit that I wouldn't see you?"

Mama chuckled. "Sometimes when I went into the bedroom in the afternoon for a nap, I really sat and knitted," she admitted.

"Well, now you've finished it. You must rest in the afternoons. It's very important," I scolded her.

"You sound like your father," Mama said.

I grimaced. Sounding like my father was not a compliment any longer, and she knew that.

"You've been so helpful to me," Mama said. "A real woman taking over so many chores. I could never have managed so well without you. Maybe when the weather gets warmer, when it's really spring and not just on the calendar, maybe then your father will—"

"Will what?" asked Papa, walking into the kitchen and kicking off his muddy boots.

"Will you have a cinnamon roll?" asked Mama. "They're special for Emma, but I know you favor them too."

Papa washed his hands at the tap and poured himself a cup of coffee to go with the cinnamon roll. And Mama's sentence remained unfinished.

The third package on the table had arrived a few days ago in the mail from Dossi. "You were out getting wood when the post arrived," Mama said. "I know it's illegal to tamper with the U.S. mail, but I guess I can be forgiven for hiding this till your birthday." I opened the little package, and inside was another leather-bound volume by Shakespeare, a companion to the one I received at Christmastime. This time the name of the play is *All's Well That Ends Well*. I like the message in that title, if only I could believe it was true.

*I* wore my new sweater to the choral rehearsal, but Cole wasn't there to see it. In fact, Josie wasn't there either. During the break I overheard Mary Wheeler talking to someone about her sister's engagement. That was news to me! My heart sank. The two absences and the news about Josie seemed to mean only one thing. I've been telling myself not to think about Cole, but I haven't been very successful. After all, he did send me a Valentine. But I guess he's as fickle as they say many men are. And who can blame him if he can't even speak with me?

This unusual spell of warm weather continues. Even at night the temperature doesn't drop below freezing. As I lie in bed, I can hear the gurgle of water from the melting snow. It drips from the roof and runs in little rivulets along the ground. And when I walked to town yesterday, I could see that the ice in the rivers is thawing. The water level is wonderfully high. The ice-skating season is long over, not that I have cared to go skating since Cole could no longer partner me on the ice.

This afternoon when Papa came in from outside, his boots thick with dark, oozing mud, he announced that the forsythia along the side of the barn was in bud.

"Already?" asked Mama. "That's amazing. We'll have to cut a few branches and bring them inside to force them into bloom. I don't remember our forsythia ever blooming before mid-April."

"We'll have another snowstorm or two yet," Papa predicted. And though none of us said anything, we all agreed. Why, we have even had snowstorms in early May once or twice in the past.

Well, tonight there was a storm, but not snow. We had a heavy rain that lasted about three hours.

"If all this water were snow," Papa declared, "we'd have another couple of feet to dig out of."

"Then thank goodness it wasn't snow," said Mama. "I've had enough."

"Me too," declared Nell. "The girls at school all want to jump rope, and we can't do that in the snow, or in the mud, either."

"Just another few weeks," said Mama. She patted her stomach. In another few weeks, she'd be nursing the new baby. Unlike Libby, who is constantly speculating on whether she will give birth to a boy or a girl and what they will name their child, Mama doesn't talk much about this new member of our family. I think she feels superstitious. After all, she's lost a couple. But I heard the doctor tell her that she was doing very well, and there was no reason to anticipate any problems.

"If we'd only known about all the snow and rain, we could have avoided digging the new well," said Tim.

Tim likes to pretend that he's lazy, but he works every bit as hard as Papa. He's never commented to me about Papa's words to Cole, but a couple of days after that incident, he came over to me when I was milking one of the cows and said, "You look pretty as a picture." I'd awakened with a cold, and so I knew my nose was red.

"Some picture," I scoffed at him.

"Any fellow who likes you will always carry a pretty picture of you in his heart," Tim said with certainty.

I knew that Tim wouldn't say more. Of course, his words could be taken two different ways. Did he mean that he'd always think I was pretty, or was he referring to Cole? But because of the timing, I was fairly certain he was thinking of the latter.

When Tim spoke of the unneeded new well, Papa said, "It won't hurt us to have an extra source of water. What with the new livestock and watering the fields, one can never have too much water on a farm."

Friday, April 5, 1912

Today it has rained nonstop. It rained all day yesterday, too.

"At this rate, we may have to worry about flooding," Papa said. And I remembered how just a few days ago, he had said we could never have too much water on a farm.

"Maybe we should begin work on an ark," suggested Tim. "It was useful to Noah, after all."

"Shhhh," said Mama. "That's blasphemy."

"What's blasphemy?" Nell wanted to know at once.

There are three streams that run through Jericho: Brown's River in the north, Lee's River

129

in the center of town, and Mill Brook to the south. All three have water to the tops of their banks, a combination of the melting snow and the intense rainfall that we've been getting for the past couple of weeks.

"I hope it isn't like 1903," Mama said.

I was only seven that year when a flood carried away a sawmill on Brown's River. I remember people talking about it more than I actually remember the event itself. Our farm is slightly elevated, unlike others, which are in the valley, so we didn't suffer. Hopefully, if there really was another flood, we would be safe again. But then I started thinking about other people we know. Eddie and Libby's land is lower than ours. And adjacent to their property is the land that belongs to Libby's father. We all pray that the rain will stop and the water level in the streams will subside to its normal height. It doesn't seem possible that the clouds can hold still more rain.

We've continued to have rain since I last wrote. On April sixth and seventh the rain still came down. On the morning of the eighth, Tim took Nell and his other passengers off to school and then he was going to do errands for Papa. But Tim returned home after a bit without having completed his tasks. "The bridge has washed away across Brown's River," he announced.

"Oh, my heavens. Why did we send Nell to school today? I can't believe that the school is in session under these conditions," Mama said. "Go back at once and get her."

"I'm going to need help," Tim said. "Emma, come with me and help me manage the wagon."

I jumped up and put on my jacket and cap. I wrapped the long scarf that I'd been knitting all winter around my neck. The weather isn't really so cold, but the constant rain quickly makes one feel chilled.

"Be very careful," Mama warned as we left the house.

Papa was coming from the barn. He wanted

to go with Tim, but I urged him to stay with Mama. "The water level probably won't rise here, but just in case there are problems, she'll feel safer with you," I said. "Mama can't move very fast these days," I reminded him.

I was surprised that he listened to me. "All right," he agreed. "I know you are both sensible and you won't take unnecessary risks. Get Nell and come straight back home."

The ground beneath our wagon was more than mud. There was at least an inch or more of water all along our route. At some points, where there were underground streams, the water was considerably higher. At one point poor Dandy let out a loud neigh as the water reached his knees. The wagon bounced along. This was our old road and, at the same time, it was not the road that we knew at all. Many rocks had been dislodged by the constant rain and there were unexpected holes. We had to watch that Dandy didn't stumble and fall in one. It would be so easy for him to break a leg. I let go of the side of the wagon and took off my scarf. I had to wring it out—that's how wet we were getting.

We passed a few homes with people rushing

about outside. Mr. Morgan was gauging the water level outside his house.

"I'm going to put as much furniture on the second floor as I can," he said. "Could you give me a hand?"

Poor Tim didn't know what to say. Mr. Morgan has only one arm. He lost the other in an accident some years ago.

"I can handle the wagon alone," I told Tim. "And when I come back this way, you can take over again."

"Are you sure?" he asked. His face was covered with rain, and his hair stuck out of his cap and lay plastered against his face. I guess I looked the same way.

"Yes. Yes," I said. "Hurry." I could see that the water level was rising.

Tim jumped off the wagon. "Let's get all your kids upstairs before you worry about the furniture," he told Mr. Morgan.

The Morgans have six children under the age of ten. The three older ones were at school with Nell. But the little ones were underfoot, and Tim hustled them upstairs. Mrs. Morgan was standing looking helpless, holding on to her favorite cut-glass pitcher, which had belonged to her mother. I've had lemonade that was poured out of that same pitcher on several hot summer days.

The wagon was full of water as I approached the center of town. I thought I'd have to get hold of a pail and try and bail some of it out before Nell could sit down. But when I pulled up in front of the school, the door was closed and the building looked empty. In fact, as I looked around through the rain, it seemed to me that the entire area was deserted. Could everyone have abandoned the town in hopes of escaping from the water?

I jumped down from the wagon and landed in water up to my ankles. I tried to pull the schoolhouse door open. It was stuck shut by mud and pebbles and was hard to manage. Finally I got it open and water rushed inside. I shouted out, but there didn't seem to be anyone there. I rushed back to the wagon and wondered where everyone was. If Nell had attempted to walk back home, I would have passed her on the road. Could she have gone home with one of her school friends? And if she had, which one? And if not, where was she?

Nell's friend Carrie lived nearest to the school. I decided to go to her house in hopes of finding Nell there. To get to Carrie's home, I had to cross the Lee's River Bridge. Unlike the wooden covered bridge on Brown's River, this was a large, solid stone bridge, and it never occurred to me that it wouldn't hold up forever. But as I approached the bridge, I had my doubts about it. The water level had already reached the bridge walkway, and I knew that the water would also have been undermining the support system. I decided not to risk taking the wagon over the bridge. Instead, I got out, and as an afterthought, I took the harness off of Dandy. Should the water flood too much, he could swim to safety if he was free. With the weight of a wagon attached to him, he would never be able to make it.

I patted Dandy and gave him a big hug. He was almost as old as me and had been with our family all his life. "I'll be back for you," I promised him. "First I have to find Nell." Dandy nodded his head and gave a snort as if he understood me. Did he remember the flood of 1903? I wondered.

I pushed the hair out from my eyes and

started off on foot. I was midway across the bridge when it collapsed. I heard the collapse before I felt it. There were loud splashes, followed by a huge shudder as the supports gave out. Suddenly I was catapulted into the rushing river water and pulled downstream by the current. It was freezing cold, and I was terrified. There were whole young trees floating around me, and I tried to grab hold of one. It wasn't easy because the weight of my wet clothing pulled me down. I kicked off my boots so I could maneuver better. I'm a good swimmer—Eddie taught me when I was little. But I've never been in any water but that of our little pond. Sometimes in the summer I swim back and forth across it as many as twenty times, which Eddie says builds up my stamina. But how can you compare swimming in a placid pond on a hot summer's day with keeping afloat among trees, logs, bits of furniture, and all sorts of other debris amid the rushing water of a flooded river? Twice I was hit by logs and went under. But each time I somehow managed to pull myself upright and grab hold of branches from floating trees. Finally I succeeded in grabbing a stout log, which probably came from the sawmill. I removed my scarf and, with great difficulty, keeping one arm around the log, used the scarf to tie myself to the log. I knew the wood would float, and hopefully so would I. And although the water was rushing along fiercely, the jam-up caused by so many logs slowed my movement along the river.

I had time to catch my breath and look around. I had never been so frightened in all my life. My face was equally wet from the river's water and the salty tears that I shed. But what could I do? I hoped Nell was safe wherever she was. And what about Eddie and Libby and the unborn baby? I shivered both from fright and cold. My toes felt like little lumps of ice, colder than they had been when I was out in the winter blizzard searching for Nell.

My teeth were chattering as I looked about for the river's shoreline. If only I could reach it! But the water level had obliterated the riverbank. All I could see was water and more water. The land looked so distant to me.

A pair of beavers swam by. It's funny that for one moment I was pleased to see live creatures. Those beavers didn't have to worry about drowning, I thought. Then I saw a cat floating past me. It was dead, and I shuddered, thinking that soon I might join it. The cat was followed by other drowned creatures: sheep, a cow, and several chickens and a chicken coop that had been dislodged by the water. I thought of poor Dandy and prayed he was safe. Hopefully he'd turned around and made his way back home. But I knew that if he arrived home without me, my parents would be distraught. Off in the distance, I thought I could hear voices. It might have been my imagination, or it could have been people who lived near the river shouting to one another. Their homes were probably being flooded at that very moment. Would the water rise beyond the ground floor? How high could the water go?

I looked again for the shoreline. It seemed so far away. Lee's River seemed to have swollen enough to take up the whole world.

I think now that if I hadn't tied myself to the log, I would have let go. I wanted to close my eyes and go to sleep. Nothing seemed to matter; nothing seemed real. Just water all around me and water still coming down from above. After a bit I realized that it was no longer raining. But I was already so totally soaked that it didn't comfort me at all.

Suddenly I was jolted alert by a voice in the distance calling out. "Hello," I heard.

At first I was certain that I was having a hallucination. Could the beavers have learned to speak?

"Hello. Hello. Can anyone hear me?"

I wanted to call out, but when I tried nothing came out of my mouth and a considerable amount of water went in. I tried at least to move in the direction of the voice. It was coming from my left, and so I kicked my feet to move that way. I stubbed my toes on a plank that was in the water. But my feet were so numb with cold that I hardly felt the pain.

"Hello. Hello." The voice was decidedly nearer.

And then suddenly, a distance away from me, I saw a canoe being paddled cautiously between the logs and the debris. A figure was steering the boat, but I couldn't make it out. Was it one of my brothers? It couldn't be my father. He was home caring for my mother.

"Hello," the man called out. "My God,

Emma. Is that you?"

This time I recognized the voice. And as the figure came nearer, my heart beat rapidly. Cole Berry had come to rescue me.

"I'm here. I'm here," I called out, and this time a sound actually managed to squeak out of my throat.

"Hang on, Emma, I'm coming."

Never in my life had I been so glad to see someone. Of course, at that moment I guess I should have been glad to see any human being with a canoe planning to rescue me. But that it should be Cole made the miracle of my rescue doubly wonderful.

Still, I wasn't saved yet. Cole couldn't reach me because of all the logs separating us. "If only I had a rope," he called to me.

"Wait," I shouted back. "Use this."

With difficulty, my frozen fingers managed to untie my scarf from the log and throw it to him. He caught it on the second try. Then, tying it around his waist, he threw the other end to me. I grabbed it, and he reeled me in like a big fish. And as I came toward him, I suddenly realized why I was knitting and knitting that scarf all winter. I must have known I would have need for a very long scarf before the summer arrived. I fell into his strong arms, very wet but saved at last.

Of course, my adventure in the flood didn't just end with the arrival of Cole in the canoe. When I got into that little boat, we still had at least an hour of paddling through the swollen river until we found the shore. It took all of Cole's energy and concentration to balance the canoe around the debris that was everywhere. So we barely spoke, not that either of us felt bound by Papa's injunction under these circumstances. And finally, when we reached land, we had to trudge through the muddy lanes, past uprooted trees and bushes, until we got to Eddie's house. I was very relieved to find Eddie and Libby safely ensconced on the second story of their house.

"How did you know where to look for Emma?" Libby asked Cole when I was sitting in the dry room with a blanket around me.

"I met Tim," he explained. "He was standing in four feet of water, where the Lee's River Bridge used to be, when I saw him. He told me that he was looking for his two sisters. I said we should split up, and I'd go along the river and he should go by land. Actually, I was able to help several people on land before I remembered that Mr. Adams had an old canoe, and I took it. And here I am."

"Here you are. You make it sound so easy," I said. "How long were you in the canoe?"

"It's hard to know when there isn't any sun," said Cole. "But I expect it was a couple of hours."

"Someday I shall buy you a pocketwatch as a thank-you for saving my life," I told him. "Then you'll always know the time."

"Finding you alive was a fine reward. I don't need anything more," said Cole, reaching over and squeezing my hand. "Besides, if I'd had a watch in my pocket today, it would have been ruined by the water. I was worried that Emma might not survive the flooded river," Cole added in a quieter voice.

"What a horrible thing to say," exclaimed Libby.

"But it's true," said Eddie. "It could have ended that way."

His words made me shudder. I didn't say anything, but I truly believe that had Cole come a quarter of an hour later, I might indeed have been drowned.

"I also managed to save three chickens," said Cole. "I pulled them out of the water and threw them in the direction of a floating tree. They say that chickens are dumb, but these three knew enough to use the wings that God gave them. They landed in the branches and hopefully are still floating along, seeing more of Vermont than they ever imagined existed."

Cole was trying to distract us with his humorous comments. But, though I had removed my wet clothing, was wearing a dry frock belonging to Libby, and had a heavy blanket around my shoulders, I still felt cold and frightened. I didn't believe I could ever feel warm again. I was also worrying about Nell and Tim. Were they safe and dry now too? And whatever happened to Dandy?

"You should have seen the huge hog that floated past me," Cole told us. "It would have provided enough ham and bacon to feed a family all winter long. Now it's too late."

"Never mind hogs," I said. "Do you think there are townspeople who lost their lives?"

"I hope not," said Cole. "The buildings were

all evacuated in the lower sections around Jericho Center. I know the schoolchildren were sent away as soon as there was word about the bridge on Brown's River. No one guessed that Lee's River Bridge would give way, too."

"I was on it when it went," I told them.

"Then it's a miracle that you survived," Eddie said. "That you are sitting here with us is thanks to God's mercy."

"And Cole's efforts," I added. One should always give credit where credit is due.

As it turned out, the floodwaters managed to reach even the higher ground where our farm is located, and there were many miracles that day. In all our town, not a single human life was lost. Nell spent twenty-four hours at the home of her friend Carrie. They were safe and dry and thought of it all as a big adventure until the water subsided and they saw the extent of the damage. One can't imagine what a flood can do until one has lived through the actual experience. I'd heard so many flood stories in the past, and they meant little more than ancient history to me. Now I know it can happen again.

Seventy townspeople found refuge in the

First Congregational church, which is located on higher ground. I don't know if they found religion that day, but they found dry blankets, hot coffee, and hundreds of sandwiches. Papa and Mama spent hours in Nell's and my upstairs bedroom together with all our chickens that Papa had managed to bring indoors. That was a major accomplishment on his part, but the mess those chickens made is something to wonder at. I never would have known they could do so much harm in so short a time. We didn't lose any livestock. All the cows survived, and even Dandy managed to make it home again. All we lost was the wagon I'd tied to the tree. (The tree is gone too.)

I learned something else that day. As we sat together staring out the window and watching the water level begin to subside, Libby told me that Josie Wheeler is going to marry Josh Merryman, the redheaded fellow that she once scolded for splashing her with mud. It was an amazing piece of news to take in together with everything else that had happened. The fact that we were all safe and well was the most important thing. But this unexpected engagement was good news too.

# JERICHO REPORTER

## APRIL 10, 1912

## Mother Nature Strikes Again

After an unnaturally dry summer, a winter of fierce snowstorms, and an early spring thaw, the people of northern Vermont have received the harshest blow yet from Mother Nature.

On Monday, April 8, three clouds, one from the south, another from the west, and the third from the northwest, came together over the area and produced an extraordinary amount of rain. In Essex Junction, ten inches of water fell in a single hour and here in Jericho, it is estimated that at least as much water fell in that same amount of time.

This heavy rain, added to the waters of the melting snows, has produced severe flooding. The local rivers, Brown, Lee, and Mill Brook, which had been so low only a few months earlier, suddenly had more water than their banks could hold. And farther away, the waters of the Dog, Otter

Creek, Mad, Winooski, and Onion Rivers have all flooded the area, causing considerable damage. House foundations have been destroyed, trees have been torn up by their roots, and numerous bridges have washed away. The sorry and pathetic sight of so many fields that are now covered with stones and boulders is grim to behold.

Residents are urged to postpone any unnecessary travel as the condition and strength of existing bridges and roads is not yet known. It is feared that still more house and bridge foundations have been affected and that there will be more collapses even after the water level has returned to normal.

As of this account, we are aware of the death of 15 sheep (belonging to George Adams of Jericho Center), and several cows and many dozen chickens and hogs belonging to the local farmers have also been lost. It is hoped that no human life was lost, but it is too soon to give full and accurate reports.

The water level has now dropped, and if there is no further rain in the coming days, we are hopeful that the floods are behind us.

# BURLINGTON
# FREE PRESS

The luxury passenger ship the RMS *Titanic*, making its maiden voyage from Southampton, England, to New York, has reportedly sunk after hitting an iceberg in the North Atlantic Ocean. There were more than 2,200 people aboard the ship when it set off on April 10. A huge number of these people have reportedly drowned due to a lack of sufficient lifeboats. An incomplete listing of the names of the known survivors is on page 4. A full count of the victims has yet to be made, but it is believed that the number will well exceed half the passengers.

During the past few days the world news has pushed our flood off the front page. The new headlines are all about the terrible tragedy that occurred when the ocean liner *Titanic* hit an iceberg and sank in the Atlantic Ocean. Fifteen hundred lives were lost. The paper is full of stories about how a wife and children got on the lifeboats and watched as the husband remained on board. Some of the victims were millionaires like Benjamin Guggenheim, Isidor Straus, and John Jacob Astor—all names I've seen mentioned in the past in Papa's newspaper. Imagine. Such an expensive luxury boat (they say it cost ten million dollars to build), and the owners scrimped so there weren't enough rescue boats for all the passengers.

Yesterday, when I went into town to the creamery with our small amount of milk, the *Titanic* was a big subject of conversation. Of course, the horrific number of people who sank with the ocean liner dwarfs the smaller drama that occurred here in Jericho. And ironically, both events involved water and drowning.

Still, there were many stories about our experiences here. There are tales of animals who apparently sensed the danger before humans. Mrs. Morgan says that the day before the flood, their cat was busy all afternoon carrying her six small kittens, one by one, upstairs to the attic, away from their cozy place near the kitchen stove.

And old Mr. Jeffers was awakened in the middle of the night by his cat jumping on him in bed. He got up and discovered that the water level on his bedroom floor was already up to his ankles. We've always kept our cats in the barn and never inside our own living area, but these two stories make me think that perhaps we should reconsider this arrangement.

There was a special thanksgiving service at the Methodist church with more people than usual in attendance, because people of all denominations came together. The ministers from the local churches took part, and I guess people wanted to hear their explanation of what we'd been through. We were so glad to see our neighbors and acquaintances, and we gave a prayer of thanks for all that we'd kept. "Don't think of losses," the Methodist minister said. "Remember what we have retained!"

Then he diverted us with some tales from the flood. "These may be apocrypha," he claimed, "or they may be true. I for one don't know."

One of the funniest stories he recounted was that of a farmer in Essex Junction who lost his barn and all his livestock and hay and feed when the floodwaters carried them off into the river. Amazingly, within the hour, another barn came floating toward his land and settled itself right where the original barn had been. After a bit, the owner of the upstream barn arrived on the scene. Seeing his barn so well placed, he conceded that he'd have to leave it there for a bit, at least until life returned to normal.

"Well," said the first farmer who had lost his barn. "It does belong here. My barn's lost, and the Lord has provided me with this one in its place."

"Gosh!" said his neighbor. "You mean you think you own my barn? Are you going to claim all the stock and what goes with it?"

"I certainly do," said the first farmer.

"They're all mine."

"In that case," concluded the upstream farmer, "if you believe that all that goes with the barn belongs to you, I'd better go home and bring down the missus and the six children!"

We all laughed at that tale, but I rather doubt that it really happened.

Everyone along my route to town was still busy cleaning the mud and silt from the ground floors of their homes and rebuilding chicken coops and sheds that had been destroyed by the floodwaters. Road crews are busily strengthening the foundations of the existing bridges, and in the months ahead, work will begin on rebuilding most of those that collapsed. Tim told me he envies Cole's chance to make his fortune. There will be good employment for him and any other independent men who go to work repairing the roads or the railroad lines.

Dead cows, sheep, and chickens are still being pulled from the rivers and are burned or buried before their decaying carcasses can spread disease. By summer I imagine most people, except those farmers who lost their homes or the most livestock, will hardly talk about the flood. Life

will just go on for us.

But even though our danger was so slight compared with the *Titanic*, I know I will never forget the nightmare of what happened here. They say that the ship was advertised as unsinkable, taunting the Lord with the ability of man over the Divine. No one pretends that we could ever control the weather. Rains will come, and floods will come again too. Perhaps we have learned a little to prepare us for the future. Perhaps not.

What have I learned? That I am stronger in an emergency than I would have guessed, that people will help one another in times of stress, and that Papa and Mama can change their minds.

Last week, when things calmed down at home, after we heard the news that Libby had given birth to a healthy, nine-pound baby boy (they're naming him Edward after Papa and Eddie), when the doctor said that Mama was fine despite all her unusual exertions and anxieties caused by the flood, then Papa and Mama took me aside for a serious talk.

"Emma," Mama said, her eyes dark with intensity. "You've been through a lot in these past few days. We've all been through a great deal. And we're lucky to have survived as well as we did. You're just sixteen, but when one lives though such dangers and acts as sensibly as you did, it is as if one has aged more than two days or even two years."

I wondered if Mama had spotted a gray hair on my head the way she was talking. (Libby already has a few gray hairs at nineteen. She claims her mother was totally white-headed by the age of twenty-five.)

I must have looked very puzzled, because Papa said, "Let me try to explain it to her."

"Explain what?" I wanted to know.

"Well, on the one hand, you're still a young girl. Much too young to think about getting married. At least not for another two years," he added.

"Yes," Mama chimed in. "Even though I was seventeen when I married your father. But we are not unaware of the fine qualities of Cole Berry. Why, he risked his own life to save yours. And he tells us he is willing to wait until you're eighteen."

I looked at my parents in amazement. When

had there been time for Cole to speak with them? I wondered.

"So we told him that although you're still too young for him to start serious courting, if he feels the same way two years from now and if you feel that way too, then we'll give you our blessing."

"Does that mean I can go ice-skating with him?" I asked incredulously. It was about the most absurd thing I could have said. The ice is long gone, and there won't be any more for months and months.

"Yes," said Mama, grinning. She, too, must have realized that there wouldn't be much ice-skating in the immediate future.

"And Cole can sit next to you in church, if you promise to keep your mind on the sermon and the readings," Papa said.

"And he can come for dinner on Sundays, if he would like to," Mama added.

"And you can change your mind at any time," Papa said. "After all, you're still sixteen."

I nodded. They say you have to summer and winter together before you know each other. And there will be many seasons ahead of Cole and me before Mama and Papa consent to our marriage.

However, I know deep in my bones that I'm not going to change my mind. It was made up months ago when Cole was working so hard digging our well for nothing but a slice of pie.

There may have been more that my parents planned to say, but at that moment Mama began to feel the birth pains of the new baby. Perhaps she'd been feeling them all during our conversation. But suddenly she let out a gasp, and both Papa and I knew at once what it meant. We helped her to the bedroom, and Papa went to call Tim, who was working in the barn. Tim hitched up Dandy and rode off for the midwife.

I spent the afternoon distracting Nell. She couldn't understand why the midwife didn't want her in the room with Mama. I suggested that we bake a cake to celebrate the birth of her new brother or sister. Nell isn't always fond of kitchen chores, but we don't bake cakes every day.

"What kind would you like best?" I asked her.

"Maple spice with vanilla icing," she said at once.

So what with cracking open nut shells and beating eggs, I kept my sister entertained. And all the while I was singing to myself: *Cole, Cole, Cole.*

And I even thought of another name: *Emma Berry*. I liked the way it sounded.

In time the maple spice cake with vanilla icing was ready. And not long afterward, our new brother was born: Simon Meade. He's smaller than Libby's son, but he'll catch up! There will be a lot of work to be done with a new baby at home and mud still clinging to the walls. But work never hurt anyone, and I know it will help the time pass quickly.

I thought about Josie Wheeler, who, according to the local gossip, will be wed the first Sunday in July. That is one piece of good news for a family that lost its sawmill and livelihood because of the flood. It is said that after her marriage, Josie will be moving with Josh Merryman to Burlington, where his uncle owns a large clothing emporium. The uncle has offered Josh a position in his store and then, as the uncle and his wife have no offspring of their own, it is believed that Josh will eventually inherit the business. Josie will like having access to all those store-bought clothes to add to her wardrobe. I hope she and Josh will be very happy together. I am glad Josie and Josh made their plans before the flood. It would be awful to think she surrendered her interest in Cole when she thought that without her father's sawmill, he would be unemployed.

Tomorrow is Sunday, and Cole is coming for dinner. I've made a vinegar pie and a dried apple one too. I wonder which one he'll like the most? Now I must make time to write a letter to Dossi. I want to tell her that Shakespeare was indeed right: "All's well that ends well."

# *Author's Note*

Although this is a book of fiction, Emma Meade and her family have become good friends of mine. Authors devise characters, and then these people take on their own personalities and behave in unexpected ways as the story develops. So, like you, I found some surprises in this book.

Emma and her family and friends are all people I have made up. But I have taken the liberty of inviting two *real* people into my story. The first is Grace Ann Goodhue Coolidge, who was born in Burlington, Vermont, and grew up to marry another Vermont native, Calvin Coolidge. Emma meets Mrs. Coolidge in 1911. I'm sure Emma will recall her, a dozen years later in 1923, when Grace Coolidge is the new first lady of the

United States and her husband becomes the thirtieth president.

The other true person referred to in this book is Wilson Alwyn Bentley, known to his Jericho neighbors as Snowflake Bentley. In 1911–12 he was beginning to gain national fame for the photographs he took of snowflakes. Emma knows him as a somewhat eccentric though pleasant individual.

The true and tragic event of the sinking of the *Titanic* is, of course, well known. It serves to remind us that at the same time that *history* is occurring, everyday life goes on. In fact, who is to know what is history and what isn't?

Among the research that I did in preparation for this book was to attend a lecture on dowsing. I attempted, and think I succeeded, to find a source of water on some property in East Dover, Vermont. Yet the subject of dowsing is controversial. Many people do not believe in the unexplainable powers of the dowser. Nowadays, though there are still dowsers who can be called upon when searching for a well site, one has the option of examining geological maps and using modern equipment that was not available to

Emma's father. They were fortunate to find a dowser who could successfully locate a source of water for them.

I attended a sugaring session when the sap was rising in the maple trees. And once again I read many books, especially *The History of Jericho, Vermont, 1763–1916*, a treasure trove of information about Emma's community that was published in 1916.

In this book I read the anecdote about a young man carrying a sheep upstairs inside a shed in order to win a bet. It's an interesting coincidence that in Laura Ingalls Wilder's *Farmer Boy* (Harper & Brothers, 1933), this very same story is related. Perhaps it is a rural legend and has been repeated elsewhere as well.

I also read old newspaper accounts from this era as well as from contemporary Internet sites that provided me with clues to life in the past.

A day for girls like Emma and Nell Meade was very different from one for girls today. There were many chores that needed constant attention: daily cleaning of soot from kerosene lamps, emptying ashes from the fireplace and wood-burning stoves, and carrying more wood into the house. In the kitchen there were no labor-saving devices like electric mixers, blenders, food processors, microwave ovens, and dishwashers. Women developed strong muscles beating, chopping, and mixing food themselves. Instead of a refrigerator, the family had an icebox, which kept food cold by the presence of blocks of ice, which were covered with sawdust and stored in a special shed. Of course, the warmth from the stove would in time melt the ice. Then one of the girls needed to empty the melted water and replace the piece of ice with another. Clothes washing was done by hand, and afterward the clothing needed to be ironed. Washing machines, Laundromats, and dry cleaning shops were far in the future.

When these chores were done, there was still more work waiting: sewing of new clothing and mending of the old. The motto Use it up, wear it out, make it do, or do without, reflected the attitude toward clothing and most other items in a farmer's home.

Even something as basic as a simple cheese sandwich, a meal we can fix for ourselves without much effort, thought, or time, would have been a major achievement for Emma Meade. First the wheat was raised on the family farm. The grain was taken to the local mill, where it was ground into flour. At home the flour was baked into bread. The cheese, too, was made at home from the milk of the family cows. The same would be true of any butter spread on the bread. Only when everything was completed could a cheese sandwich be made and eaten.

But finally, when work was over, Emma and Nell could read or write by the light of their kerosene lamps or candles. They could do knitting or fancy needlework. And they could even play games: There were simple, often homemade toys (batteries didn't exist in those days), card and word games, jacks, pencil and paper activities such as cut-out dolls, and other pastimes. And on a crisp winter day or evening, they could go outdoors and enjoy ice-skating or sledding, just like you.

Almost a century has passed since the period in which this story is set. Yet although science has developed so much to simplify housework, communications, and travel, and has conquered so many medical problems, some things have not changed. Every year the world is full of devastating fires, earthquakes, floods, tornadoes, hurricanes, tsunamis, and other natural disasters that we still cannot control. The peaceful rural life that Emma and her family know is almost destroyed by the flood that I have written about in this book. Although in actuality there was no drought in the east during the summer of 1911 and no major flood in northern Vermont in 1912, I was thinking of several floods in other years: 1830, 1849, 1914, and especially the one in November 1927, when many lives as well as buildings, bridges, roads, and trees were lost. It's considered *poetic license,* and not bad history, when a writer of fiction plays with facts and dates, and even the weather, as I have done in this story. *Lights and Shadows of the Flood of 1927* by Charles T. Walter and Zenas C. Jenks, which was published in 1928, provided me with much information about that flood as well as the folklore that grew up around it.

In Wilmington, Vermont, where I spend my summers, there was a severe flood on September 21, 1938. To this day there is a painted marker in the center of the town that indicates the amazing

166

and frightening six-foot-high water-level mark of the flood. All these years later, the line reminds townspeople and visitors to the area alike about the powerful force of nature. At the same time, this dark line inspires viewers with knowledge about the strength and determination of humans to rebuild and continue despite devastation.